The Adulterers

LAWRENCE BLOCK
writing as Andrew Shaw

THE ADULTERERS

LAWRENCE BLOCK writing as ANDREW SHAW

Copyright © 1960 Lawrence Block

All Rights Reserved.

Cover and Interior Design by QA Productions

A LAWRENCE BLOCK PRODUCTION

CLASSIC EROTICA

21 Gay Street
Candy
Gigolo Johnny Wells
April North
Carla
A Strange Kind of Love
Campus Tramp
Community of Women
Born to be Bad
College for Sinners
Of Shame and Joy
A Woman Must Love
The Adulterers
Kept
The Twisted Ones
High School Sex Club
I Sell Love
69 Barrow Street
Four Lives at the Crossroads
Circle of Sinners
A Girl Called Honey
Sin Hellcat
So Willing

CLASSIC EROTICA #13

THE ADULTERERS

Lawrence Block

Chapter 1

The road from Freer to Laredo is sixty miles of absolutely nothing. The road is straight as a die and flat as a pancake and about as stimulating as a seventy-five-year-old wart hog with pimples on her nose. For sixty miles the Texas sun beats down on you and the road stretches out in front of you and the desert extends on either side farther than you can hope to see, and the only redeeming feature of the monotony of it all is that the sixty miles takes a good deal less than an hour to drive. There are no gas stations to fill up at, no rest rooms to unload at, no hot dog stands to get ptomaine poisoning at. There is, in short, absolutely nothing from Freer to Laredo, and as soon as you pass Freer you press the accelerator pedal to the floor and release it only to come into the town of Laredo.

Not that Freer is such a town to write home about, for that matter. Not that the whole state of Texas is such a big deal, when you stop to consider the question. In fact as far as George Sutton was concerned they could take the whole mess—every bloody oil well and every last clump of tumbleweed or whatever the hell it was—anyway, they could take it and stick it in Alaska or something.

George Sutton fished a handkerchief out of a pocket and wiped sweat from his forehead. He noticed a spot of something or other on the horizon and decided that it must be Laredo. It couldn't be much of anything else. There simply wasn't anything else. It would be Laredo, and that meant that he and Mona could get the hell out of that hotbox of a car and get the hell into an air-conditioned hotel room.

Which would be a pleasure.

"Laredo," he announced.

Mona Sutton, who was sitting as far on her side of the seat as was humanly possible, didn't say anything. She had nothing to say. Well, that wasn't quite it. To be more precise, she had nothing to say to George Sutton.

George Sutton was forty years old, looked forty-five and felt fifty. In New York he worked from nine to five Monday through Friday thinking up clever notions for the advertising firm of Romberg and Clay. In return Mr. Romberg and Mr. Clay paid George Sutton enough of a living so that he could afford a home in Westport that was damn near paid for, an Oldsmobile that was all paid for, and a beautiful young wife who would never be entirely paid for.

Which, obviously, is where Mona comes into the picture.

Mona was twenty-four and looked twenty-four, which is a fine age for a woman to be and a fine age for a woman to look. Mona had long hair a little lighter than gold and a body which, while slim and supple where it was supposed to be slim and supple, was as big as the state of Texas in other places.

Which, all things considered, was one of the main reasons George Sutton had married her.

"Laredo," he said again. Mona nodded vacantly and seemed to shrink against the door on her side of the car. To hell with Laredo, she thought. She closed her eyes and tried to get her mind focusing properly.

How did it happen? You were a beautiful girl from South Orange, at least everybody told you that you were a beautiful girl, and you went on being beautiful and carried off prizes in some of those simpy beauty contests and went to New York to be a model. And all this time, all through high school, all the way to New York and modeling and all, all this time you never let a man touch you.

Well, hardly. Sure, the boys were buzzing around all the time. And they made passes—clumsy passes but passes just the same. And, naturally, you let a guy kiss you now and then. If a guy took you out on a date and he was a nice guy and you liked him, then why in hell shouldn't you let him kiss you? And, for that matter, you let one of them touch you. Just a little, but the fact remains that he touched you and you liked it. He was a boy named Bruce Pillson and he took you out dancing at the Red Mill and you both drank a little beer and when he stopped the car in front of your house and kissed you, you kissed him right back, and when he touched your breast you didn't jerk away.

She closed her eyes, remembering. Bruce's hand had been very gentle as if he was afraid her breast would burst if he held it too tight and she liked the way he was holding her, liked it very much. And when his other hand lifted the hem of her dress and slid up her leg to the soft sleek skin on the inside of her thigh she liked that even more.

And then he was touching her, his fingers warm and hungry and probing through the silky panties that were so thin that they didn't do much good at all, and oh Jesus God how nice it was!

But that was all that happened. And she never went out with Bruce Pillson again. And nobody ever touched her, not from that night on.

Until George. She shook her head groggily, wanting to drift off to sleep but unwilling to let the train of thought slip away from her. George saw her when she did her first modeling job for Romberg and Clay, took her out for dinner that night and to a Broadway show the following night, proposed two weeks later and married her within a month.

Met her.

Took her out for dinner.

To a show.

Married her.

And then, God help us, made love to her.

She tried to keep from shuddering. George was a good man and he loved her, for a starter. And she loved him, which only made everything that much worse.

Because she and George were about as compatible as oil and water. From the honeymoon on, going to bed with George was an experience that started poorly and got progressively worse, until now the two of them avoided it as much as was humanly possible.

George put a cigarette between his lips and pushed the lighter into the socket on the dashboard. After a few seconds it popped out and he touched the end of it to the tip of his cigarette, drawing hot smoke into his lungs. He blew out the smoke in a cloud and eased up on the accelerator as the car neared the city limits of Laredo.

He let go of the steering wheel with one hand, took the cigarette from his lips and sighed. Out of the corner of his eye he took a long look at his wife. It wasn't exactly a hungry look. In a way it was the look of a penniless kid with his nose up against a candy store window. Except in this case the kid couldn't get in.

Not quite. Not quite, he decided. He could get in easily enough. It was just that once he got in he wouldn't be hungry any more.

He looked at her again. Big bulging breasts that looked even better without the flimsy blouse she was wearing. Big ripe breasts that didn't need a bra to keep them looking good. A milky complexion and the softest skin in the goddamned world, skin as good as the skin in the soap ads. A spider waist. Hell, she was all sex-stimulation from head to toe and topped off with the most beautiful mop of hair in captivity.

Beautiful, he thought. *A beautiful bitch. Hello, you beautiful bitch. Why are you so rotten in bed, huh? What makes you such a lousy lay?*

He dragged again on the cigarette, then wiped more perspiration from his forehead and swore silently to himself. Well, it was his own damned fault. If he had had any sense he would have banged her before he married her. You didn't buy a car without driving it around the block a few times, did you? So why in hell marry a woman without taking her out for a ride?

He shook his head. Well, he told himself, it was different with Mona. He met her and he fell in love with her and he wasn't just looking to get in her pants. From the moment he met her he knew he was going to wind up married to her. He'd done enough helling around. He was thirty-six years old and ready to settle down; she was twenty years old and ripe for plucking. It seemed incredibly simple at the time.

So they got married and drove way up into Northern Vermont and took a cabin in the woods. Then he got the clothes off of that unbelievable body of hers and then the world started to go quietly to hell. He damn near had to rape his own wife on his wedding night, and if that wasn't one hell of a state of affairs he didn't know what was.

A virgin. Now how a girl with a face and figure like she had managed to stay a virgin for twenty years . . .

Well, so she was a virgin. That was her business. But the bitch was *still* a virgin and she would be a virgin forever, no matter how many times he made love to her. She would just go on lying on her back like a slab of cement while he worked away, and when it was all over she would be as cold as she had been when it started.

Four years. Four years without a decent piece. Well, that wasn't entirely true—there was the time when he stayed late at the office and made it with one of the secretaries on the couch. A nice skinny little brunette with hard little knobs and a motion like a pogo stick, a sexy little number as hot as a pot-bellied stove.

Yeah, that was nice. He didn't have to get down on his knees to get *that* one on her back. Nothing like it. All he had to do was give her a smile every morning for a week, pat her behind once or twice, ask her to stay late and then stick his hand up her dress after the rest of the crew was home for the night. And the minute he touched her the little minx was on fire. The minute his hand was playing games with her she was crawling all over him.

Wham.

Bam.

Thank you, Madam.

•   •   •

The sign on the road said:

WELCOME TO LAREDO
DRIVE CAREFULLY

"Welcome to Laredo," George said, half to himself and half to Mona. "Drive carefully."

And, of course, she didn't say anything. They hardly so much as talked to each other any more. They stayed in their own beds and kept to themselves. He went to whores or found something on his own or had wet dreams for himself. He could just look at Mona and get excited, but all he had to do was lay a hand on her and he might as well be rubbing a piece of ice.

He shook his head, angry at himself for being too hard on her. Hell, she tried. It wasn't as though she was cheating on him— small danger of that. And it wasn't as though she didn't want to be good in bed. She just didn't feel a goddamned thing, that's all.

Well, this vacation of theirs would settle it. They had a whole month to spend in Mexico, and during that month one of two things would happen. If they were lucky, the change of scene and change of pace would result in a change in Mona. There didn't seem to be much of a chance of it, but with a little luck maybe she'd be able to relax and enjoy sex. And if that happened George Sutton would be a contender for the title of Happiest Man in the World. He was married to the world's most beautiful woman, and if the marriage would only work out the way it was supposed to everything would be all right.

But that was a slim chance at best and he had to admit it to himself. No, the odds were that Mona would finish out the vacation as sexless and unresponsive as she had started it. And if that were the case they wouldn't be married when they got back from Mexico. It would be a nice clean break—a quickie divorce in Monterey and back they'd go to New York. He'd sell the house in Westport and take an apartment in the Fifties, and the first thing he would do was stock the place with a good houseful of liquor and shack up with a hot little sex machine who would know what to do when the lights were off and who could loosen up and enjoy it. She wouldn't look as good as Mona, but they all looked the same in the dark. What was the French saying—something about all cats being grey at night.

He pulled the car up at the first gas station he came to, filled the tank and got directions to the Plaza. It was supposed to be the best hotel in town and he felt like getting a good night's sleep.

He parked the Oldsmobile in the hotel lot and took the two suitcases from the trunk. Then he opened the door for Mona.

"Come on, honey," he said. "Let's get checked in."

She got out of the car dutifully and walked at his side, across the door and through the lot and into the lobby. The desk clerk was a scrawny red-necked Texan with a wad of chewing gum in one corner of his mouth and he took a long time looking Mona up and down. Then he turned to George and gave him a quick wink.

George felt like laughing out loud. It was obvious what was going through the kid's mind. He thought Mona was somebody George had picked up for a pleasure trip, probably figured her for a high-priced professional. George felt like telling the kid how wrong he was, then changed his mind. He signed the register, gave the bags to a bellhop and followed the bellhop into the elevator.

In the room he said: "We can get a bite to eat if you're hungry."

"I'm not hungry. We ate in . . . where was it?"

"Freer."

"That's it," she said. "We ate in Freer. That was just a little while ago."

"An hour or so."

"What time is it now?"

"Ten o'clock."

"I'd just as soon get to sleep, George. I feel all gritty from the driving and I'd just as soon take a good shower and get to bed."

"Okay."

"We can get an early start tomorrow."

He shook his head. "Have to get tourist cards and clear out all the red tape—it may take a day or two. The town across the river's supposed to be fairly lively in the meantime."

"Can we go there without tourist cards?"

"Yeah. There's a strip of land along the border that's under Mexican jurisdiction but it's the same as if it was the United States. You can go close to sixty miles into Mexico without a tourist card. That's what keeps the border towns alive—American tourists crossing over to drink or gamble or find a woman."

"What's the name of the town?"

"Nueva Laredo. It means New Laredo."

She nodded. "We'll go there tomorrow," she said. "You take your shower first while I get our stuff unpacked—I might as well get everything out if we're going to be here for a couple of days."

While he was undressing he noticed that the clerk had given

them a double bed instead of twin beds and he was angry and amused at the same time. After a look at Mona the red-necked bastard took it for granted that George would want to be in the same bed with her. He didn't even take the trouble to ask. Well, the hell with it. No point in making a fuss. He could stay on his side of the bed and she could stay on her side and the hell with it.

The shower felt good. Driving over the desert was not only tiring but dirtying as well and he felt a good three pounds lighter after his shower. He put a fresh blade in his razor and shaved quickly and precisely, thinking that he'd have to shave again in the morning anyway at the rate his beard grew. But he hated to go to sleep with stubble on his face.

He wrapped himself in a towel and left the bathroom. She was in her robe and she passed him without a word, walking into the bathroom and shutting the door behind her. He heard her start the water running and he thought Now she's taking the robe off, now she's all nice and naked and now she's stepping into the tub, now the water's hitting her and making her skin glisten and now she's rubbing that hunk of soap over those breasts and that golden bowl of a stomach and . . .

He sat down heavily on the edge of the bed. She had left a half-empty pack of cigarettes on the night table next to the bed and he lit one, trying to draw in enough smoke to get her off his mind.

It didn't work.

He stood up and walked across the room, throwing a switch and plunging the room into darkness. Then he went back and sat down again on the edge of the bed and smoked the cigarette. He listened to the water in the bathroom and imagined what she looked like taking a shower. Maybe he could go in and watch her while she showered. Maybe he could turn into a Peeping Tom and spy on his own wife. That would be a brand new perversion for a married man. That would be a hell of a note. There were enough guys his age who didn't sleep with their wives because they just weren't interested in their wives any more, but he was damned if he knew anybody who was going through what he was going through. It didn't make sense.

He grinned involuntarily, then leaned over and ground out his cigarette in the ashtray on the night table. That damned fool of a clerk! It would be a hell of a lot easier if they were sleeping in separate beds tonight. One more night of her next to him and him scared to touch her because he was afraid she'd cringe away from him and he'd go out of his mind.

Although she didn't exactly cringe. It wasn't as if his touch sickened her, at least not at first. At first it had just been that she was unmoved by the whole procedure. Then, as the months passed, she resented his ardor as much as he resented her lack of it.

Pretty soon they wouldn't be able to stand the sight of each other.

He raised the covers and got under them. The room was air-conditioned and the air-conditioning made it cold enough so that a blanket was necessary. The air was cool and clean and the bed was soft and the pillow softer. He rested his head on the pillow and closed his eyes.

It ought to be easy to sleep, he thought. He was tired, there was no question about that. He was exhausted, as a matter of fact.

He was a New York City boy and he wasn't used to driving, and in the past few days they had done one hell of a lot of driving.

It ought to be easy to sleep.

But it wasn't.

Not at all.

Not with the shower going in the other room. Not with hot water pouring down on the most beautiful creamy skin in the world. Not with the most desirable woman ever just a few yards away from him.

It was impossible.

He pulled the covers over his head and tried to get away from the noise of the water. His mind started to reel and he thought that the water would come down for forty days and forty nights. He better get to work building an ark. He'd make it the right number of cubits high and the right number of cubits deep and the right number of cubits wide, and then he'd get a pair of each species of animal . . .

Sure.

If I was Noah, he thought, *the human race would die out. I'd get the damned ark built, all right. That would be easy enough. And I'd get all the damned animals on it, and then I'd get on it along with Mona. That wouldn't be too hard to take care of.*

But then, after the whole shebang landed on Mount Ararat, then everything would go to hell. They wouldn't be able to be fruitful and multiply. Not Mona. She was as useless for having babies as she was for sleeping with. She was good to look at but that was about all.

He felt himself relax and his breathing became slower and more rhythmic and he thought: *In another minute I'll be asleep.*

Just another minute, just one more damned minute and I'll be asleep.

And then, inevitably, the water stopped running in the bathroom. The sudden silence was so loud that he sat bolt upright in bed, every muscle tense, every nerve standing on end and screaming in matching silence.

She hopped out of the tub and reached for the towel, hoping that he was asleep by now, thinking that he just had to be asleep or she would go crazy. If he was awake he would want her and she knew it, knew the depth of his desire just as surely as she knew the lack of her response to it.

Nothing.

A big blank nothing.

It wasn't his fault. At first she had thought that he was responsible for her own inadequacy, that there was some tragic flaw in his lovemaking that made it meaningless to her. But she knew that it wasn't his fault.

She proved this fact to herself the hard way. She proved it by taking another lover a little over a year ago. The man in question was a neighbor, a Westport dentist, and while she managed to avoid the classic suburban Man Next Door stereotype, Herb Pomerantz was as close to that stereotype as you could get. He made love to her a total of four times—that was all. That was enough to convince her that she was no more likely to respond to another man than to George.

She toweled herself dry with a Hotel Plaza towel. The towel was too small to do the job properly and she thought that there had to be some hotel in the world where the towels were large enough. Hell, this was Texas, wasn't it? Wasn't everything supposed to be big in Texas? Then why were the towels so small?

She looked at herself in the mirror and she told the reflection: *You're hedging, honey. You're dodging the issue. You're sitting on the pot and refusing to get off, because while you're babbling mentally about towels there's a whole area of human experience of which you are painfully ignorant.*

The reflection gaped foolishly.

You, she told the reflection, *are nothing more or less than a frigid bitch.*

But why? She wanted sex, wanted it with a dull ache that no amount of frustration could thoroughly submerge. When she married George she took it for granted that the two of them would have a thoroughly satisfactory sexual relationship. She went on her honeymoon as eager for physical love as any other bride. What went wrong?

First there was the fear. It made her tense and tremulous and all tied up in knots while George was making love to her. Then there was the pain, the terrible terrible terrible pain when he did it to her, the pain that lasted all the while.

Now she was over the fear.

Now there was never any more pain.

There was nothing.

And the constant eternal nothing was infinitely worse than all the fear and pain in the world.

She folded the towel and hung it on the towel bar. Her robe was on the hook where she had left it and she reached for it, actually had it in her hand and off the hook before she changed her mind and decided to leave it there. Tonight she wouldn't wear a robe. Tonight she wouldn't wear anything.

Tonight she would be sexy.

Sexy. The word had a humming sound to it, a sound of profound activity. And she had to be profoundly active, damn it. Or otherwise the unstated purpose of the Mexican venture would be fulfilled.

In which case she would find herself divorced. A Mexican divorce, to be sure. But a divorce.

And, if their bedroom problems didn't iron themselves out, she'd *want* a divorce. She'd want it as much as George did. The way things were going now they were just driving themselves crazy.

She opened the bathroom door. The light from the bathroom cast a hazy glow around her bare body as she walked, hips swinging, from the bathroom to the side of the bed.

He watched her every step of the way. He watched her, his eyes caressing every perfect curve of her perfect body, and he wanted her more than he had ever wanted her before.

God, he thought. Maybe it was going to work. Maybe the change in climate was going to make for a change in Mona. Maybe . . .

He lay very still in the bed, only his eyes moving to follow her as she came closer and closer. Neither of them said anything and she walked softly so as not to wake him, but it was a game and both of them knew that it was a game. She knew damned well that he was awake; he knew that she knew; she knew that he knew that she knew and so on. Well, let her play her game. If it made things better for her, that was her business. It was certainly working on him. He felt himself trembling with desire.

She walked to her side of the bed and lifted the covers, slipping under them and resting her head on her pillow. He still didn't move. He could smell the warm female smell of her bare skin fresh from the soapy shower and it sent an extra shiver of desire through him.

A whisper: "George—"

He didn't move. He was afraid to move, afraid to spoil the almost magical perfection of the moment.

A shade louder: "George—"

He rolled over toward her. Their bodies were as close as they could get without touching and the smell of her was strong and exciting in his nostrils.

Go slow, he told himself. *She's trying, she wants to be good for you, she's doing her damnedest. Be gentle with her, go slow, be good to her.*

He took her in his arms and kissed her. Her body pressed against his and her full and perfect breasts were warm against his chest. He caught his breath, overcome by the sheer physical magnificence of her.

But at the same time he couldn't help detecting the undercurrent of tension that ran through her.

Steady, he thought. If only she could relax. If only she could just let go and abandon herself.

He kissed her a second time, thrusting his tongue out and forcing her lips apart. Her mouth opened to admit him and he caressed her lips and tongue with his tongue. The kiss lasted a long time while he tasted the warmth and sweetness of her mouth. Then he released her.

His hands found her breasts and cupped them. He held the sweet flesh in his hands, caressing her, loving her, trying valiantly to excite her. But it wasn't working. Her nipples hardened and stiffened automatically when he pinched them but he knew that this was nothing more than a reflex, an inevitable response to tactile stimulation.

He put his mouth to each of her breasts in turn, running his tongue over the satiny skin. A small moan escaped her lips but he knew it was an act, an attempt to make him happy. He couldn't help being pleased that she was trying, couldn't help it any more than he could prevent the aggravation that he wasn't succeeding in arousing her.

Easy, he thought. Maybe if he just took his time, if he made it go slow enough.

He cupped her round buttocks in his hands and squeezed them. His fingers traced a course over her hip and down to the downy skin on the inside of her thigh. His fingers stroked her there and moved up to the special part of her that he loved so much. He touched her there and she twisted and writhed on the bed but even as he abandoned himself to what he was doing, even as he touched her and kissed her he knew that she was feeling nothing, that his caresses were not exciting her in the least.

Easy, he thought. Easy.

But he couldn't wait another minute. His own passion had mounted to uncontrollable heights and he couldn't take any more time for preliminary lovemaking. Greedily, urgently he flung himself upon her and took her, needing her, craving her, moving with her in the timeless rhythms of love.

Her body moved the way a woman's body was supposed to move. Her legs wound around him and her arms tightened around his back. She said his name once, making it sound almost like a prayer, a supplication to a higher power. Maybe that was what it was, he thought sickly. A prayer that he would finish up and let her get some sleep.

He kept moving with her, kept loving her, and for the slightest second he was lost, completely lost in the depth of his love for her. But the moment passed in a flash and his climax was quick and fitful and unsatisfactory—and horribly alone.

He released her, rolled free of her. He gave her a final kiss and saw that there were tears in the corners of her eyes. She opened her mouth to say something but her mouth went shut again before any words had come out.

"It's all right," he whispered, knowing as he said it that it was not all right at all. She knew, too, but his words calmed her and she nodded. Her eyes closed.

He rolled over on his back, exhausted without being fulfilled, sated without being satisfied, empty of everything but his omnipresent feeling of emptiness. She had tried, tried valiantly, tried to please him and to please herself. She was a good woman, a sweet woman, a wonderful woman.

Just before he drifted off to sleep he thought of the way she had said his name and made it sound like a prayer. That was a neat trick—*George*, when you came right down to it, wasn't the most exciting name in the world. But she had turned it into a prayer.

What the hell, maybe he ought to pray. Maybe he ought to

ask God to turn his wife into a sexpot. You never knew what was going to work and what wasn't—that was a cardinal principle in advertising.

Maybe he should try a prayer. Maybe he should run it up the flagpole and see if anybody saluted it.

He almost laughed. Praying was as stupid a notion as he had ever come up with. God would almost give a damn what his wife was like in bed.

And, incongruously, he remembered the line from *The Naked and the Dead*:

If there's a God, he's a son of a bitch.

Chapter 2

He knew it was morning when the rays of sunlight came through the window and stabbed through his closed eyelids. He rolled over away from the sun, then gave up and opened his eyes. Mona was already up and dressed; he could hear water running in the bathroom now and it reminded him of the way the water had been running the night before.

He took a deep breath, let it out and reached for the pack of cigarettes on the night table. There was only one cigarette left and he lit it, crumpling the empty pack into a ball and flipping it toward but not into the waste basket. The first drag on the first cigarette of the day was strong in his lungs and made him a little dizzy for a moment or two. The second drag tasted better.

He kicked off the covers, sat up on the edge of the bed. Before anything else he strapped his wristwatch onto his wrist and discovered that it was almost a quarter after nine. He had slept long. He wondered how long Mona had been awake, guessing by the number of cigarettes that were gone that she had been up for two hours at the very least. Then he set his cigarette down in the ashtray and dressed. He put on a short-sleeved pale blue sport shirt and a pair of lightweight grey gabardine pants.

The water stopped running in the bathroom. Then the door opened and Mona appeared. She was wearing slacks and she was the type of woman who could get away with it. She looked good in slacks. Hell she looked good in anything—or in nothing at all.

"Good morning," she said.

"Is it?"

"Isn't it?"

He shrugged. "You might call it that, I suppose. My mouth tastes like a cesspool—I better brush my teeth. You have any breakfast yet?"

"Not yet."

"You must be hungry. How long have you been up?"

"A couple of hours. I'm not sure exactly—I didn't even notice what time it was."

"Let's go out for breakfast."

She nodded and waited while he washed up and brushed his teeth and combed his wiry brown hair. Then she took his arm, looking for all the world like the dutiful and loving wife, and they left the room and took the elevator to the main floor. George noted with pleasure that the red-necked desk clerk wasn't on duty.

There was an inexpensive restaurant at the corner of Fourth and Grand which the elevator boy had recommended and they had scrambled eggs with home fries and bacon and strong black coffee. They shared a cigarette with coffee and it helped get George fully awake.

"Well?"

"Well, what?"

He ground out the cigarette in an ashtray that was big enough for a dozen cigarettes and that seemed to symbolize the mental outlook of the whole state of Texas. Everything was so goddamned big.

"Well," he began again, "what do you want to do today?"

"I don't care."

"First we might as well apply for the tourist cards. Good thing to get that out of the way. Nueva Laredo's supposed to be interesting but it's just one of those border towns like Tijuana and Juarez and we'll probably get tired of it in a day or two. Sooner we get the tourist cards the sooner we can push on into the interior."

"Meaning Mexico City?"

He nodded. "Mexico City especially," he said. "A few other spots might be worth hitting—Monterey, maybe. Acapulco, except this isn't the tourist season there and it may not be too exciting. And side trips to places like Cuernavaca and Taxco, of course. But especially Mexico City."

"To find the lawyer?"

He winced.

"Well, isn't that what we're going there for?"

He took his time before he answered her. "I don't know," he said. "God knows I don't want a divorce. I love you, Mona."

"I tried," she said. "I tried awfully hard."

"I know it."

"I tried my best. I wanted it to happen, George. And I wanted you to make love to me last night."

"I know."

"But—"

He shook his head. "Forget it for now," he said. "Maybe everything'll work out. Let's just go get the tourist cards and then find out what Nueva Laredo has to offer."

•　　•　　•

The man at the Laredo Chamber of Commerce was helpful. He explained, first of all, that one did not get tourist cards at the Laredo Chamber of Commerce. One went instead to the office of the Bureau of Tourism in Nueva Laredo. He also explained that there were money changers located on both sides of the border who would happily convert American money into Mexican currency when one crossed into Mexico and reconvert Mexican money to American when one returned to the States.

But, he added, and George shouldn't say he said so, there was no point, in the world in converting money until he got into the interior, since American money was as interchangeable and exchangeable as Mexican in Nueva Laredo. "It's all geared to the American tourist," he explained. "The town lives on Americans. And you don't have to try to speak Spanish—even the kids speak English."

They thanked him and left, taking with them one of the usual helpful booklets that told you things you should have known to begin with—such as: Don't make fun of Mexicans; Don't drink water south of Monterey unless it's the bottled pure water; Don't sneak firearms across the border. They walked from the Chamber of Commerce to the bridge that spanned the Rio Grande, paid ten cents to the guard on duty at the bridge and started across. When they reached the other side they were officially in Mexico.

"We're in Mexico," she said. "That's funny. I don't feel any different. You would think I would feel different, being in a foreign country."

"Haven't you ever been out of the States before?"

"Never."

"I was in Canada a few times," he said. "And over to Europe

once, but that was during the war and I don't suppose it counts as foreign travel."

She shrugged and didn't say anything.

The main street of Nueva Laredo confirmed the words of the man at the Chamber of Commerce. Everything was aimed at the American tourist market. In addition to the rows of money-changers there were rows of liquor stores, rows of junk jewelry shops, rows of the usual tourist traps that sold imitation alligator bags, uncultured pearls and grubby pillows that said "Souvenir of Nueva Laredo" on them. George wondered idly why anyone would want a grubby pillow as a souvenir of Nueva Laredo. Maybe to stick under his mate's hindquarters while he gave it to her, he guessed.

And then, while they were walking quite aimlessly, a little boy came up to prove that all the stories about all the border towns were quite true.

"Hey, Joe," he said. "Wanna lay my sister?"

The fact that Mona was present seemed to make no difference to the boy. He was perhaps ten years old. George gave the kid a half-hearted smile.

"Joe," the boy persisted, "my sister only twelve years old. She virgin, Joe. Everybody say she good lay."

George laughed. He noticed out of the corner of his eye that Mona was grinning.

The kid didn't give up. "You got cigarette for Papa, Joe?"

George gave him a cigarette. The kid smiled broadly and put it in his mouth.

"Got light for Papa?"

George lit the cigarette for him. The kid took a healthy drag on the cigarette, inhaled like a trouper and ran off down a side street.

"For Papa," Mona said. "Sure."

"His Papa was probably an American tourist and his Mama probably earns her living horizontally. What of it?"

"He shouldn't be smoking, not at his age. It'll ruin his health."

"So what?"

She looked at him, puzzled.

"What does the little bastard have to look forward to? So he smokes now and it takes five lousy years off his lousy life. You think it makes any difference?"

"Maybe you're right."

"Of course I'm right," he said, strangely irritated. "Does it matter if he lives fifty years in poverty or sixty years in poverty?"

"You don't have to shout at me."

"I'm sorry."

They found the office of the Bureau of Tourism. It was a singularly unimpressive building, a large wooden frame affair that resembled an unpainted barn more than anything else. They waited on an uncomfortable bench until a girl took their names. Then they waited again until the girl brought cards for them to fill out.

"Occupation," George read. "What the hell difference does it make to them what I do for a living?"

"They probably want it for the record."

"What record?"

"I don't know."

"I'm going to put down Garbage Collector," George said. "The hell with their record."

She shrugged.

"Religion," he read. "Well, I'll be damned. I don't see why the hell it's their business what my religion is."

"Probably—"

"Don't tell me," he said. "The goddamned record. Put down Zen Buddhist, will you?"

"What for?"

"Just put down Zen Buddhist. It'll puzzle the hell out of them. I bet they never got a pair of Zen Buddhists before."

She shrugged again.

They waited again and he decided that the major occupation in the country of Mexico was waiting—waiting for Lefty, for Godot, for *mañana*, for the reappearance of Ambrose Bierce. All the goddamn time you had to wait.

"Señor Sutton?"

The Mexican official had a pencil-line moustache and slickly combed jet black hair. He smiled as if his face never knew another expression.

The official took their papers, checked them briefly. When he got to *Religion* his eyes lit up. "Zen Buddhists," he said. "We seem to get more of you people every day, Señor."

"You do?"

"More every day," the official said. "Most of them younger than yourself, and most of the young men seem to have beards like Fidel Castro. It must be the coming religion in your country, *verdad*?"

"Yes," George said, weakly. "It's quite the thing now."

The official's smile widened. He had said something very perceptive and he was obviously pleased with himself. "Your cards will be ready tomorrow, perhaps the day after. You will call for them?"

"Certainly," George said.

They left.

"Zen Buddhists," Mona said when they were outside. "He got us mixed up with the beatniks."

"Yeah."

"Well, that was a new one."

For some reason, no reason he could put his finger on, everything she said was suddenly annoying to him. Her remarks were friendly and innocuous enough but they got on his nerves nevertheless. He felt like telling her to shut up.

"I'm sorry," he said suddenly, without really having done anything to be sorry about. It was as though he was saying that he was sorry for everything, everything that was wrong.

"I'm sorry," he repeated. And he took her hand in his and squeezed it with a mixture of love and agony.

Every Mexican town has a plaza. Most of them have a good deal more than one plaza. Nueva Laredo had several but one was more important than the others. It was in the center of the town, a large grassy square lined with benches.

It was seven-thirty. They were sitting on one of the benches, sitting together without speaking. They had managed to kill the afternoon without doing anything, having a shot of tequila, which they didn't like, at a bar just off the plaza; having rum-cokes, which they did like, at another bar.

They drifted back to the American side for dinner and had

steaks in the very good restaurant at the hotel. Then, because there was nothing special to do on the American side, they paid their dime once again and wandered across the Rio Grande to Nueva Laredo.

If they hadn't done this they might never have made the acquaintance of Ernesto.

He was a very little man with sideburns and the perennial pencil-line moustache. He approached them directly and smiled graciously.

"May I sit with you?"

George told him it was all right with them. He sat down next to George and turned to look at both of them.

"I am called Ernesto," he said. "I am a guide."

George nodded.

"I am not what you call a gyp artist," he said. "I am licensed by the Department of Tourism as a guide. If you like I show you my license."

"It's all right," George said. "We believe you."

"Here," Ernesto said. "My license." And he produced a license which made absolutely no sense to George because he could not read a word of Spanish. But the license certainly looked impressive enough.

"Stop me if I offend," Ernesto said. "You are married, *verdad*?"

"We are married."

"And this is your first time to Mexico?"

"That's right."

"And you wish perhaps some excitement?"

George shrugged. "Depends what you mean by excitement,"

he said. But he had an idea what Ernesto was leading up to. He couldn't keep all the interest from showing in his voice.

"Some attractions we do not have in Nueva Laredo," Ernesto said. "The jai-alai, that you will find in Mexico City. The bulls— we have bulls here, but the better bulls and the better toreros are to be found farther south. You would be wise to wait to see the bulls."

George didn't say anything.

"But other attractions," Ernesto said. "Marijuana, for example, is illegal in Mexico. It is not permitted. But if you wished to obtain some marijuana—"

"Sorry," George said. "Not interested."

"I thought not, and I hope you will not take offense. I only felt I ought to mention it in case there was an interest. Perhaps you might want to see a show?"

George's pulse quickened but he tried to keep it from showing. He wondered whether Mona knew what the guide was talking about.

"What kind of a show?"

"It is very delicate," Ernesto said. "You will not be perhaps offended if I speak directly?"

"Go ahead."

"The show is very exclusive." He pronounced it *esclusive*. "It is several men and several women. Do you understand?"

"I understand."

"It is not, how you say, vulgar. Some shows that some of these guides would take you to, hundreds of people stand together and watch. That is not nice."

"I see."

"But this show," Ernesto went on, "this show is private. There are others watching, but they watch from private *compartamientos*. Completely private."

"I see. How much does it cost?"

"It is a long show," Ernesto said, hedging. "It will begin in perhaps a half hour. It will last for two, maybe three hours."

"How much does it cost?"

"One hundred dollars."

"One hundred dollars American?"

The Mexican nodded. "That is for a *compartamiento*," he explained. "And of course you may retain the *compartamiento* afterwards for as long as you wish it. There is no extra charge for it."

George took two cigarettes from his jacket pocket, offered one of them to Ernesto. He lit them both with his lighter, then said: "Will you permit me to discuss this with my wife for a moment?"

"Of course, señor." Ernesto stood up and walked away, taking a seat a few benches off.

George drew on his cigarette. "You know what he's talking about, honey?"

"I think so."

"He means a sex show."

"That's what I thought."

"You know what it is, don't you? You have a compartment to yourself and they perform on a stage and then you do what you want afterward."

She nodded.

"I've never been to one. Would you like to go?"

She shook her head.

"Why not?"

"I just wouldn't, that's all."

"You might like it. You might get excited—I don't know."

"I don't want to go."

"Well, if you're not going to give yourself a chance, how in hell—"

She looked at him.

He didn't say anything.

"You want to go, don't you?"

He shrugged, then nodded.

"You want to go even if I don't go, don't you?"

After a moment he nodded again.

"It's all right," she said. "You can go by yourself. I don't mind."

"I'd rather go with you, Mona."

"No," she said. "You go. I'll have a drink here and meet you back at the hotel."

He thought about it for a moment, then nodded and waggled a finger for Ernesto. The Mexican returned.

"My wife won't be coming," he said. "I'll go alone."

The Mexican's face remained impassive. "Certainly," he said. "The fee is still one hundred dollars American for a *compartamiento*."

"That's all right."

"You will come with me? It is not far."

"All right," George said. He glanced briefly at his wife, then took a breath and stood up. Ernesto started walking away and George followed him, overtaking him after a few steps and walking along at his side.

She remained on the bench until they were out of sight. Then she took a cigarette from her purse and lit it, wondering whether in Mexico a woman was considered a tramp if she smoked in public. She decided that she didn't really care what she was considered. She felt like smoking and she was going to smoke, and if they didn't like it they could take their dirty country and shove it.

So George was on his way to a sex show. Hi ho, hi ho, it's off to the Mex sex show. Well, if that was what he wanted, let him have his fun. It was, to use a common American colloquialism, no skin off her ass.

Or was it? She wondered idly whether it might not have been better if she went along with George. God knew how little she wanted to see a sex show, but at least it would have kept peace in the family. Or, to be more precise, it would have kept the piece in the family. Because it was a sure thing that George wasn't going to just sit there and watch and then come home when it was all over. He'd have a girl, and he'd be all hot from the show and he and the girl would do all the things they'd been watching and . . .

She took a deep breath and held the air in her lungs as long as she could. Then she flipped the butt of her cigarette into the street and stood up from the bench. She walked away from the plaza quickly with firm and even strides and didn't stop walking until she came to a small tavern on the main street of the town.

The tavern was not the one she and George had been to before. It was more dimly-lighted and somewhat higher class. She noticed that there were only a few patrons present and that they were all men. Only two were Americans.

She walked into the tavern and took a table near the rear. The waiter who came to serve her spoke excellent English and brought her a rum-coke right away. She paid him and took a sip of the drink. It tasted good.

She closed her eyes and tried to imagine what George was doing. The show would be starting in a few minutes. Men and women would do things on a stage, things she couldn't even begin to imagine. And then George and some dark-skinned Mexican girl would do things.

Well, would it have been any better if he was doing them to her instead of to the prostitute? Would it have been such a bowl of cherries if she and George had been squirming around in some dinky little *compartamiento*, some grimy cubicle with the sweat of former occupants imbedded in the carpet? He would be hot as hell and she would be cold as ice, and what good would it do?

George was selfish, she decided. He was leaving her to satisfy himself.

Then she changed her mind. George wasn't selfish. He had wanted to bring her along, because he thought it might excite her. She was the selfish one. She wouldn't even give it a try. She was just a frigid bitch with an icebox between her legs instead of a furnace.

She ordered another rum-coke and drank it straight off, then signaled for a refill. Midway through her third drink she got to wondering about the icebox between her legs. She knew that it had been there last night—she had used it last night, or at least George had used it. But maybe it wasn't there any more. Maybe it had atrophied from lack of use.

Well, she really ought to find out whether she still had it. It wasn't much good to her, but it would be sort of silly to go through life without an icebox in the usual place. She glanced around vaguely to see if anybody was watching her. Nobody was. Then she slipped one hand under her dress and ran her hand up her thigh to her panties. She slipped one finger under the elastic at the base of her thigh and poked around until she found what she was looking for.

Well, it was still there. Thank God for that much.

Thank God for little things.

Which, being the punchline to a joke, made her giggle to herself.

Useless thing, she murmured, poking with her finger. *No good to anybody. Might as well sew you up and to hell with you, useless thing.*

Suddenly she yanked her hand away from where it was, thinking that things had gotten to a hell of a state when she had to sit around in a Mexican bar and play with herself. *This calls for a drink*, she told herself, and she swallowed the rest of her third drink and ordered a fourth.

The drinks were getting to her. Before she had finished her fourth she felt the beginning of a glow coming over her and by the time the drink was finished she was happily numb. She wasn't used to drinking much. George was, of course—the picture of an ad man wasn't complete without the standard martini. But she had never been much of a drinker and two drinks was generally her limit.

She had had four.

But she felt fine, all things taken into consideration. She stroked her cheek and discovered that it was numb, but what harm was there in a numb cheek? She certainly didn't feel woozy or stupid. As a matter of fact she felt more intelligent than usual. She had a better perspective on everything and the world was a whole lot clearer.

On the strength of that she ordered a fifth drink. But she didn't gulp it all down at once. Instead she took a tiny ladylike sip from it and set it on the black Formica table in front of her and stared at it. What a delightful way to drink Coca-Cola! With the rum in it, one didn't even object to the fact that the coke rotted one's stomach out. It was marvelous.

What was George doing now?

Screwing, she answered herself. Screwing some pig of a Mexican, some sow, to be more precise. Screwing her silly, screwing her blind, screwing her until her thing was good and sore. Maybe George's thing would be sore, too, and then he wouldn't bother her any more at night until it was better. Maybe George would catch syphilis and they wouldn't be able to sleep together any more. That would be a blessing from the saints, it would indeed.

She took another sip of her drink and didn't even notice the man who sat down opposite her. Then she put the glass down again and now she saw him, saw him quite clearly although he seemed to be a little blurred around the edges. He looked like a Mexican in a western movie, with eyes as black as his hair, piercing eyes that blazed out of a deeply-tanned face. He wore a moustache and the ends of it were curled upward ever so slightly in a handlebar effect.

His shirt was black with black buttons, his pants were black, even the buckle on his black leather belt was black. His shoes were black and the laces were black and even his socks were black.

She said the only thing she could think of, which happened to be: "Are you really there?"

"I am here." He had a very slight accent.

"Thank God," she said. "I was afraid I was seeing Mexicans or something."

"May I buy you another drink?"

She started to tell him that she didn't much care one way or the other, but before she said anything at all he had signaled the waiter for another round.

"Who are you?" she asked.

"I am El Tigre." He said it as though that explained everything.

"Is that supposed to mean something to me?"

"It will," he said.

His teeth flashed in a smile.

CHAPTER 3

George hoped that the place wasn't too much farther. They had already walked a good ways from the center of town and the neighborhood they were in was a good deal less impressive than the downtown area.

Maybe, he thought fleetingly, they weren't going to a sex show. Maybe they were merely walking to some deserted spot where Ernesto and some friends of Ernesto would club him over the head and lift his wallet. They might crack his skull for him while they were at it. He tried to dismiss the thought but a creepy feeling remained and he couldn't shake it off. What the hell—maybe it was a good thing Mona hadn't come along. This way even if they cracked his skull open she would be all right.

He shook his head. Why hadn't she come along? That was the main reason he had wanted to go. He thought that the excitement of the show might be enough to loosen her up so that she would be able to enjoy it when he made love to her. But she wouldn't go, not Mona, not Miss Lovely Ice, and now he was stuck following some crazy Mexican to a sex show he didn't want to see in the first place.

Well, he admitted, that wasn't altogether true. In spite of himself he was looking forward to it all, anticipating it with a fast pulse beat and moist palms. He couldn't help wondering what the people on the stage would do, what they would look like while they were doing it. He was breathing hard and having trouble keeping up with the guide who was walking at his side.

"We are almost there," Ernesto said. "Another block, two perhaps. Then we will be at our destination."

"Fine."

"You will wish to watch the show alone, señor?"

George thought that one over. Somehow the whole aspect of what he would do once he got to the show had eluded him and now he had to think it over. Ernesto, evidently, was offering to provide companionship. Companionship might be interesting—strange that he himself hadn't thought of it, that it remained for the guide to raise the question.

"If you wish company, señor, it can be arranged."

"What sort of company?"

"There is a girl," Ernesto said.

"Yeah?"

"*Sí.* She is quite young, quite *simpatico.* She will watch the show with you if you wish it."

"What does she do?"

"Whatever you wish, señor."

"How much will it cost me?"

"Fifty dollars, señor."

Fifty bucks—plus a hundred for the compartment came to a yard and a half. A lot of dough. He could afford it but that didn't alter the fact that it was a lot of dough.

"She will remain for all the night," Ernesto coaxed. "She will do whatever the señor wishes and as often as the señor wishes. She is a very beautiful girl, señor."

"Tell me about her."

Ernesto shrugged. "What is there to tell? Her hair is black and glossy, her body is well formed. She has seventeen years."

Seventeen—in the States they threw you in the jug for getting into something that age. George tried to look as though he was thinking it over but he knew that his mind was already made up. A hundred and fifty bucks was a lot for a night, but it would be well worth it.

"All right," he said. "All right."

"It is at the corner," Ernesto said. "The big gray house on the corner."

The big gray house on the corner stood a ways off from its neighbors. George looked it over carefully, trying to find some way in which it looked like what it was. To him it looked just like any other stucco house, larger than most, with iron bars on the windows and a massive iron door. They approached the door and George saw that there was a peephole in it. It looked like a speakeasy held over from Prohibition.

An eye peered at them through the peephole. The eye recognized Ernesto.

The door opened.

Ernesto said something in rapid-fire Spanish and the neat young man in the neat brown suit answered in equally fast Spanish. George couldn't catch a word of it. Ernesto answered something and the neat young man said something else. George gave up trying to figure out what they were saying and glanced around the house.

The decor was typically Spanish-American but George was willing to bet that the average Mexican's home didn't come up to the furnishings of the place. There was a carpet on the floor that was thick enough so that they probably had to run a lawnmower over it once a week to keep the nap down. The several pieces of furniture that he saw were all matched and all obviously expensive. There was a painting on one wall that looked like an Orozco; if it was, it had cost somebody a hell of a lot of pesos.

The opulence of the house was reassuring. If nothing else, it meant that he didn't stand much of a chance of getting conked over the head. People with this kind of dough wouldn't waste their time with idiotic games like that. They were playing for bigger stakes.

Ernesto turned to him. "One hundred fifty dollars American, señor."

George nodded and reached for his wallet. He counted out a hundred and fifty clams in tens and twenties, noting that the transaction left him ten bucks to get back to the hotel with. Well, he wouldn't need more than that.

Ernesto took the money and passed it to the neat young man. "He will take you," Ernesto said. "He will show you to your *compartamiento*."

"What about the girl?"

"She shall join you. Her name is Letitia, señor. She does not have any English. Is that agreeable?"

George nodded, thinking that he didn't expect to carry on much of a conversation with the girl anyway. "Thanks," he said. "Thanks very much."

Ernesto nodded. "It is my pleasure," he said. "If you wish my services again you may contact me in the plaza. If you have friends coming to Nueva Laredo you may tell them to contact me there."

"Okay," George said. He started to offer his hand to Ernesto, then changed his mind. It didn't seem particularly proper to shake hands with a pimp, which, when you came right down to it, was a rather accurate description of Ernesto's duties. He was a pimp with a license from the government to prove it.

The neat young man opened the door; Ernesto walked through it and the door closed behind him. The lock clicked into place.

"You will come with me?"

George nodded and followed the neat young man in the brown suit. They walked down a hallway, turned into another corridor and kept going on a circuitous route that reminded George vaguely of the legendary catacombs. At any minute he expected Roman legions to chase him around the intricate passageways.

"We are here," the neat young man announced. He pressed a button and a door opened. They walked into a room ten feet square with a velvet covered mat on the floor and an easy chair near a window.

"The window is one-way glass," the neat young man explained. "You can see out but no one can see in."

George nodded, thinking to himself that this was probably an explanation designed to ease the consciences of the squeamish. He strongly doubted that the window was one-way glass and cared less. Just so long as he could see out of it he didn't care who saw into it.

"The girl will join you in a moment," the neat young man said. "The show will start in approximately ten minutes."

The neat young man vanished suddenly and the door closed

behind him. George sat looking at the closed door for a minute or two, then walked to the chair and sat down in front of the window. He was surprised to see that the stage was only a few yards from the window. Other windows faced his; the little stage was entirely surrounded by compartments which were probably filled with excited watchers. And, evidently, the neat young man had been telling the truth about the one-way glass. George couldn't see into any of the other compartments.

I'll be damned, he thought. *Theater-in-the-round.*

He wondered vaguely whether he was supposed to remove his clothing now or later. He decided to wait. It might be awkward to be sitting stark naked when the girl walked into the room.

And, seconds later, the girl walked into the room.

She was quite beautiful. Her skin was the color of honey and her hair was the color of coal. She wore a plain blue silk kimono that hid her body from his view but he knew from the way she walked that it was a good body. Then she closed the door and walked over to him, her eyes shining and her pretty little behind swinging with each step she took.

He didn't move. He couldn't have moved if he had wanted to and he didn't want to anyhow. He sat still in the chair while she knelt down on the mat at his feet and began to take off his shoes and socks.

He looked into her eyes. She was young enough to be his daughter and the expression in her dark flashing eyes was as old as the proverbial hills. He didn't know how to react; all he could do was speak her name: "Letitia."

She raised her eyes, smiled. His shoes and socks were off now and she was leaning against him, her tiny fingers busy with the buttons of his shirt. He felt himself getting excited already. She slipped his shirt off his shoulders and her fingers teased the mat of dark hair on his chest. It took an effort to remain motionless but he managed it.

She took off his trousers, his underwear. He was naked. She stood up and in one motion removed her kimono and let it fall to the floor. He saw that her body was the same delicious honey color from head to toe. Her breasts were small but perfectly formed and the nipples at their tips were an extraordinarily bright red. He wondered if she touched them up with lipstick or if they were naturally that color.

He started to reach for her. She grinned and sat down on his lap. She grinned at him and pointed out of the window.

The lights were going on around the stage. The lights in his own compartment dimmed correspondingly until he could barely see the soft shadows of the girl he was holding in his arms.

The show was starting.

She wasn't sure just how many rum-cokes she had had. It was very difficult to keep count, especially with this man called El Tigre sitting across the table from her and looking at her constantly with such a weird expression in his eyes. She tried to pin down his expression but she couldn't decide exactly what it was. He seemed very sure of himself, very confident. And yet there was something in his gaze, a gaze that never left her face and never wavered in its uncompromising intensity, that seemed akin to hunger.

Hunger.

Was the tiger hungry?

Now why would the tiger be hungry?

More important, what was the tiger hungry for?

"Mona," El Tigre was saying. "Mona is a very lovely name. May I call you Mona?"

"Sure."

"The name suits you. It suggests beauty and you are very beautiful."

His spots were showing, she thought. Or was it the leopard that had its spots showing? It was very difficult for her to keep them straight. Well, his claws were showing, that was what it was. She wondered if he would scratch her.

"What do you do?" she demanded.

"I already told you, my little Mona."

"Am I?"

"Are you what?"

"Your little Mona."

"Of course you are."

"Then tell me again."

He sighed, then sipped his drink. "I am a businessman," he said. "I buy things, I sell things. Occasionally I exchange things."

"And you make money?"

"A great deal of money."

"And you're a Mexican?"

"Partially," he said. "My mother was a Mexican girl with a good deal of Castilian blood in her veins."

"And your father?"

"Was a Texan who raped her."

She shivered.

"Don't be alarmed," said El Tigre. "If you consider it, it is a good thing that my father raped my mother. I bear him no ill will for it, my little Mona. If he hadn't done so I would not be here with you now. I would not exist."

"Oh."

"Oh," he echoed. "And you are waiting for your husband, my little drunken Mona?"

"I'm not drunk."

"No?"

"No."

"Not even a little bit tipsy?"

"Well," she conceded, "maybe a little. And you're right about the other thing."

"What other thing?"

"About waiting for my husband."

"Ah, yes. Your husband. You said his name is George?"

She nodded.

"George," he repeated. "A name full of romance and mystery and intrigue."

She made a face.

His eyebrows went up. "You do not find his name to be filled with mystery and romance and intrigue?"

She shook her head.

She said: Your name is filled with . . . with what you said."

"You think so?"

She nodded solemnly.

"And do you find me to be a mysterious and romantic and intriguing creature?"

She nodded again.

"My little Mona. You always say the right thing, my sweet.

Why don't you come with me and wait for your husband else-where?"

"Where?"

"At my home."

She thought that one over for a minute. "We couldn't do that," she announced.

"No?"

"No."

"Why not?"

"Because."

"That is not much of an answer, my little Mona."

She pursed her lips and thought about it some more. "Be-cause," she said carefully, "my husband wouldn't know where to look for me."

"Precisely."

She looked at him.

"That is the beauty of it," he explained. "Your husband wouldn't know where to look for you."

"Oh."

"You see?"

"I see."

"Well?"

She shrugged and he pushed his chair back from the table as if to get up. She touched his arm and he sat down again and looked at her.

"Something is the matter?"

"Nothing's the matter."

"Then let us go."

"Not yet."

"Not yet? When, then?"

"In a minute or two," she said. "Why don't you buy me another drink first while we're waiting?"

"Waiting for what?"

"Waiting for another drink, silly. What else?"

"Oh," he said. He crooked a finger and the waiter appeared with another rum-coke on a tray. He paid the waiter and handed her the drink. She drank half of it in one swallow, belched gently, and downed the rest of it in another long and noisy gulp.

George felt beads of sweat breaking out on his forehead. His palms were damp and his breathing was coming fast and hard. His eyes were fixed on the stage.

A woman was on the stage. She had appeared suddenly and unexpectedly through a platform from beneath the stage. She was tall, with dark brown hair that cascaded over lightly tanned shoulders and fell to her waist.

She was naked.

George stared at her breasts. They were huge and they were too heavy to jut out sharply but hung slightly. The effect was no less stimulating. Slowly, sensuously, the woman swayed the upper half of her body from side to side. Her heavy breasts moved like huge ripe fruit on a swinging limb. George watched in fascination. It was not only what he was watching that excited him; the fact of watching a spectacle, the notion of observing something forbidden, served to heighten his excitement.

The woman began to move her hips in the same sensual,

animalistic fashion. She turned around and around to give all the watchers a look at her.

The woman threw back her head and laughed. The laughter came through the window harsh and clear. The woman said something in Spanish and somebody else laughed.

Then she cupped her pendulous breasts with her hands and thrust out her hips insolently. Her fingers played with the dark red nipples and the nipples jutted out from the manipulation.

She laughed again.

With one hand he stroked her belly. George watched, wild with desire. He put one hand on Letitia's thigh, and Letitia wriggled and covered his hand with her own, pressing the hand in place, and moaned softly.

The woman continued to turn around and around, letting everybody see what she was doing. Then the trapdoor in the center of the stage came up again and a man appeared.

He was a small man. His long black hair was plastered down on his skull with grease that glistened in the spotlight. His chest was matted with thick black hair and there was hair on the backs of his hands and on his arms.

He walked toward the woman.

The woman smiled. She bent down and kissed the small man squarely on the mouth. Then she straightened up and wrapped her arms around him. She was much taller than he was and his mouth came right between her two huge breasts.

The short man took each of her large breasts in turn and did something to them with his mouth. The woman shrieked in passion. She rubbed herself up against him and he got excited.

George decided that his excitement was quite understandable. To say the least.

The woman pushed the man away. She planted both of her feet squarely on the wooden floor. Her feet were about a yard apart on the floor.

George was panting audibly. He took one of Letitia's breasts in his hand and squeezed it. In return she placed a hand on his chest and trailed it downward slowly past his stomach. He wanted to grab her, to take her swiftly and decisively.

And at the same time he couldn't take his eyes off the window.

The woman bent backward, slowly, languorously. She kept going until her hands touched the floor. Her back was bent and her hair trailed along the floor. The man stepped between her parted thighs. George didn't know what to do, whether to watch them or to turn his attention to the girl in his arms. But the girl settled things for him. She positioned herself in the chair so that she was kneeling over him, facing him. Her arms went around him and her soft body closed in on him. She knew what she was doing. She was making it possible for him to watch and to make love to her at the same time.

George put his arms around her. He could smell the cloyingly sweet cheap perfume that seemed to be oozing out of her tender young flesh.

He held her very close.

His body moved in rhythm with hers.

And all the while he watched what the man and woman were doing in the middle of the stage.

•   •   •

It was cooler outside.

The night was dark. The air was tropically warm but a breeze that tossed her blonde hair kept the warmth of the night from seeming as warm as it was. They walked out of the small tavern and down the street. El Tigre had his car parked down the block and he held the door open for her.

The car was a Cadillac. On the outside it was black; inside the upholstery looked to her like the skin of a tiger.

"The upholstery looks like tiger skin," she said brilliantly.

"It is."

"Really?"

"I had it made specially," he said. "Do you like it?"

She nodded and sank into her seat. He walked around the car and got in on his side. The ignition key was on a golden chain that hung from his belt. He fished it out and fitted it into the ignition. The car started at once and he pulled away from the curb and drove south and west.

She was almost too drunk to realize how drunk she was. Her head spun dizzily and her mouth tasted dry. She licked her lips to moisten them but it didn't do much good and her mouth still seemed like the inside of an old sofa pillow. Her teeth felt as though they were encased in white wooly sweaters.

She wasn't sure where they were going. Oh, yes now she remembered. They were going to his house, wherever in the world his house was.

Why were they going to his house?

She sat up suddenly in an effort to clear her head but it was too much for her and she slumped back in her seat again. Then she let herself fall toward him a little until her head rested on his shoulder. Out of the corner of her eye she saw the smile spread on his face.

The car purred like a giant cat. Like a tiger, she thought drunkenly. Like El Tigre. But why were they going to El Tigre's house? George would never find her there, and when George came back from his silly sex show he would be all worried because she wouldn't be at the hotel waiting for him. And it wouldn't do to make George worry. That wouldn't be a nice thing at all.

"Hey," she said. "Take me to the Plaza."

"To the plaza? What for?"

"The Plaza Hotel," she explained. "Not the park. The hotel across the border."

"Why? I assure you that my house is far more comfortable."

"But—"

She forgot what she had been about to say. He went on driving and she stopped worrying.

El Tigre smiled. He was feeling very pleased with himself and he was looking forward to what would happen when he had the blonde American woman to himself at his home. In the privacy of his own home he would be able to enjoy himself to the utmost, and that would be good. Very good. He always enjoyed himself when he had an American girl to enjoy himself with.

Not that Mexican girls did not afford a man a tremendous amount of pleasure. To begin with, he found the average Mexican girl a good deal more attractive. Of course they were at their best only when they were quite young. The life they led quickly told on them—their young breasts lost their savor with the passage of years, their faces were creased by lines and wrinkles and their bodies became less desirable. But when they were young they were delightful.

He turned a corner, noting with approval the way the Cadillac held to the road. Ah, yes—Mexican girls were a delight. But there was a sense of triumph in possessing an American girl, especially a golden-haired prize like the one beside him. It was exciting, inspiring, satisfying. It was, almost, as if he was exacting a delicious revenge upon the northern country for the rape of his mother by his Texan father.

The blonde girl beside him mumbled something and he took one hand from the wheel to stroke her hair. How soft it was! He wondered idly if all her hair would be as blonde and as soft. He hoped that it would.

It was, El Tigre decided, a wonderful thing to have money. The fools and romanticists who prattled that money could not buy happiness did not know what they were talking about. Money quite definitely did buy happiness. Without money what would he be? A peon. A pig, a thief perhaps—a useless toiler of one sort or another without a home or a car or a beautiful blonde woman to sleep with. Without money he would not be El Tigre, and he greatly enjoyed being El Tigre.

It was indeed fortunate that he had money. In short, it was fortunate that a large percentage of the *Norteamericanos* needed to put a needle of heroin into their arms several times each day. It was also fortunate that a far larger percentage of *Norteamericanos* took so much delight in smoking the harmless weed, marijuana, and more fortunate still that the foolish *Norteamericano* government had made the weed illegal.

The heroin and marijuana that flooded the United States came, for the most part, through the Mexican border towns—Cuidad Juarez, Tijuana, Nogales, Piedras Negras, Matamoros and Nueva Laredo. While no single syndicate could control the full deluge of the traffic, there was one group of clever men who handled a large portion of the trade.

And in each of the border towns there was one man who represented that syndicate, that powerful and wealthy organization. The man in Tijuana was known as Ranchido. Luis Chingador was the man in Ciudad Juarez. There was such a man in each of the towns.

The man in Nueva Laredo was El Tigre.

He smiled softly, remembering the early years, the struggle to organize, the job of bribing the police to look the other way. He remembered the fight to get to the top of the heap, the persuasion, the bribes, the violence. He had killed men—perhaps the clearest sign of the violence of his life was that he no longer knew how many men he had killed or had caused to be killed. The number was unimportant now. Death was an accepted fact, violence was a part of life. And he preferred it that way.

It had all been worth it—the killing, the struggling, the long lean years at the beginning. Now he had a home that was a palace and a car that was a joy to drive. He had the money and the power which could bring quick satisfaction to all the eccentric cravings that he had developed over the years. He was a man of strange passions, passions the average pig of a peon would never know, never dream about as he slept in filth on his pallet on the floor. And those passions were easily satisfied.

He whistled softly, thinking of what he would do with the

blonde *Norteamericana*. He turned the car into a driveway and pressed a button on the dashboard and the garage door opened. He parked the car in the garage and opened the door.

The house was set off in the country. The smells of Nueva Laredo did not reach it, the stench of the peons could not disturb him. That was another of the pleasures of money.

The blonde woman appeared to be sleeping. He got out of the car and her head started to slump forward; then she jerked awake suddenly and looked at him through hazy eyes.

"Where are we?"

"At my house," he said gently. "Come."

"What for?"

He reached over, patted her cheek. More familiar gestures would come later. Now he could afford to be reserved, affectionate.

"Come," he repeated. "We have things to do."

"What kind of things?"

He smiled. "Things you've never dreamed of," he said.

CHAPTER 4

One the stage the tall woman with the large breasts and the short man had finished what they were doing. The sweat that covered their bodies shone in the spotlight. The woman had collapsed to the floor and was breathing like a spent racehorse. The man lay limp in her arms, gasping like a large fish stranded in the middle of the Sahara Desert with no water for miles.

In the compartment George and Letitia had likewise finished what they were doing. George was exhausted; he leaned back in the massive chair, his head spinning, his emotions strangely tangled. With one hand he stroked the soft flanks of the exciting young girl who relaxed in his arms like a soppy dishrag. Her skin was silk-soft under his hand and he went on stroking her lower back and buttocks without giving the action much thought.

It had been an experience, to say the least. Letitia herself was an experience, but the combination of Letitia's very tangible love-making and the visual and auditory stimulation of the pair in center stage was almost too much to bear. He was physically sated, yet he couldn't get rid of a disturbing feeling of inner guilt. It was as if what they were doing and what they had been watching was essentially a private thing, a thing not designed for a public performance. This made it all the more exciting, but at the same time it left a bad taste in his mouth.

Well, he thought, it was over. He had seen a sex show. He had seen it, and it was over, and now he and the soft little bundle of sexiness would stay in their compartment until they were both totally and irretrievably exhausted. Letitia would be fun to get exhausted with—that was certain.

His mind suddenly went to his wife and he wondered what Mona was doing. The thought of her brought back the guilt feelings stronger than ever but he forced them out of his mind, forced himself to forget about her. To hell with her—she could have come along. He had wanted her to do so, had actually urged her to accompany him. She'd made her bed—now it was his turn to get laid in it.

I have seen a sex show, he thought. *And now the sex show is over.*

This is what he was thinking.

A moment later, however, he discovered that he was wrong. The sex show was *not* over.

It was just beginning to get rolling.

On the stage the man heaved a sigh and stood up. He took the woman's hands in his own hands and drew her to her feet. She shook her head dazedly and her hair flew from side to side. Then she cupped her heavy breasts in her hands and looked down at them and giggled softly.

The trapdoor opened once again.

George stared. He didn't believe it at first, didn't believe the image that his eyes relayed to his brain. He stared like a man in a trance as the girl came up through the trapdoor and onto the stage.

She was a girl, not a woman. She couldn't have been more than fourteen if she was that old. In contrast to the man and the woman she was fully dressed in a pure white dress that covered her from her neck to her ankles. Her feet were bare. They were very small and white.

The trapdoor closed and the girl stood in the center of the stage, looking lost and bewildered. She did not look as though she belonged there. She looked pure, virginal, innocent. George wanted to shout to her, to tell her to get off the stage before something horrible happened to her.

The man and woman had come to attention now. Their eyes were on the girl and the expression in their eyes was frightening. It was easy to see what was going to happen, easy to realize now what was next on the program.

It was the woman who acted first. Her hips swinging seductively she approached the girl. The girl took a step backwards but she couldn't get away from the woman.

The woman reached out a hand. Her fingers fastened upon the material of the girl's dress at the throat. Then the woman's hand moved downward like a striking serpent. In one motion she tore the dress from the girl's body.

There was nothing under the dress.

Nothing but the girl. Nothing but a soft young body, nothing but small white breasts, nothing but a flat belly and succulent thighs framing a triangle of wispy brown fluffiness. The girl's face was a mask of terror. She looked as though she was ready to scream. Her mouth was open and she was trembling like a leaf.

The woman laughed.

It was an unreal laugh, a laugh like chalk squeaking on a blackboard. The woman's whole meaty body shook as she laughed. After a moment or two the short man joined in the laughter and the three of them formed an unreal tableaux in the middle of the stage—all three of them naked, the man and woman howling like maniacal hyenas and the girl shaking like a quaking aspen in the center of a tornado.

Then the woman reached for the girl. The girl couldn't resist and the two of them fell to the floor. The girl lay on her back and the woman crouched over her. The woman pressed a kiss on the girl's small mouth. Then she trailed kisses on the girl's shoulders and down to her throat.

Her hands closed around the girl's breasts like the talons of a hawk. Her mouth moved lower and she began to kiss the girl between her breasts. Then her mouth worked on each breast in turn. Her tongue coursed over the satiny skin and her lips closed around the tiny rosebud nipples.

George couldn't stop watching. This was perversion, out-and-out perversion. It was sickening, horrifying, too much to stomach. But in spite of his revulsion he was fascinated. He was sweating profusely and he was having trouble getting control of his breathing. Without realizing it his fingers knotted around the buttocks of the girl in his arms so tightly that she squirmed in pain.

On the stage the woman was still busy with the girl. She was behaving like a man now, stroking the breasts of the girl like a lover stroking the breasts of his beloved.

Unable to restrain herself any longer the woman threw herself upon the girl. The heavy breasts of the woman were squashed against the soft little breasts of the girl. The woman's mouth fastened upon the girl's mouth and their bodies churned together. Then, suddenly, the woman straightened up.

She jabbed one finger into the girl's soft belly and the girl screamed blue murder.

The woman laughed. Then the man joined once more in the laughter. Then the woman started all over again, her mouth busy with the girl's breasts, then moving downward to kiss the sore red spot on the girl's belly where she had jabbed her. Her hands rubbed the girl's thighs as her mouth moved downward.

George watched what the woman was doing. He watched, and when Letitia slipped from his arms he was powerless to prevent her from leaving.

But she was not leaving. She was a clever girl, and even if she spoke not a word of English she knew what to do to please a man. She knelt in front of him and did what she knew he wanted her to do while he tangled his fingers in her curly hair and stared transfixed at the spectacle on stage.

She did not understand exactly what was happening. They were at El Tigre's house but she was unsure just why they had come there. Something about what a joke it would be on poor George when he returned to the hotel and she was not there—but she didn't know what it was all about.

She shook her head and her brain seemed to dash back and forth within the confines of her skull. She was alone in a room, and further inspection revealed that it was a bedroom. It took a little looking to realize this, and it wasn't just because she was drunk. The room didn't look much like any bedroom she had ever been in before.

For one thing, there was the bed. Now, the one article of

furniture that identifies a bedroom as such is a bed, and for that reason El Tigre's bedroom had her quite thoroughly faked out at the start. There was a bed, but it took her awhile before she realized that the low round thing was a bed and not some unique variety of Mexican footstool.

It was about a foot and a half high and as round as a dinner plate. It stood square in the middle of the room with nothing but space around it, and it occupied a good deal of space itself. The diameter of the circular thing was a good ten feet. The only way that she figured out that it was a bed was by the process of elimination. What in the world else could it be?

But, she thought, that was not really proper. Why, when a man met a girl it wasn't nice at all for him to take her to his bedroom. The living room, perhaps. That was the normal place to entertain a guest.

But the bedroom—

She shifted from one foot to the other, waiting for El Tigre to return. Shifting from one foot to another was not easy with the amount of alcohol in her bloodstream and she decided that it would be a good idea to sit down. But there were no chairs in the room.

She sat on the bed. Moments later music began filtering through the room, apparently coming out of the walls. Then, a few seconds after the music began to play, a door opened and El Tigre entered the room.

He was not smiling now. He was dressed in black again but he was now wearing a black silk robe and nothing else. His mouth was a thin line and his eyes were fierce.

He said: "Take off your clothes."

She stared at him.

"Take off your clothes. When I give you a command you should not sit and gape like a pregnant cow. Take off your clothes!"

She stood up, her legs shaky. It was beginning to occur to her just why he had brought her there, just why they were in the bedroom.

"Hey—"

"Hurry."

She shook her head. "You don't understand," she said. "I . . . I must have had too much to drink. I mean . . . I'm married. My husband went somewhere and I just wanted to have a drink or two and go back to the hotel."

His eyes stabbed at hers and she wanted to turn away from the force of his gaze. She managed to go on talking.

"I have to go home now," she said. "I . . . I . . . well thanks for the drinks. Maybe we can get together sometime but I'm afraid—"

He was walking toward her.

"Look," she said, "I don't know what went wrong but I maybe said something before that gave you the wrong idea. If I did I'm sorry. I guess you think that I'm here to sleep with you but I'm not because the only man I sleep with is my husband and I don't even do that too often because . . . look, I'm awfully sorry. You're a nice guy and—"

"I'm not a nice guy."

He was inches away from her.

"Look, maybe you're a nice guy and maybe you're not a nice guy—I don't know. All I know is that I have to get back to the hotel because my husband will be waiting for me and if I don't get back he'll start to worry and I don't want him to worry because that wouldn't be good and—"

"Shut up."

He didn't raise his voice. He didn't have to. The force of his words, the venom in his tone was enough. Involuntarily she backed away. She took half a step; then the bed was pressing against her calves and she couldn't back up any more. She was afraid now. She didn't know why but she was scared, scared stiff, scared as she had never been scared in her entire life. One time she had been out driving with a boy and another couple and the car had gone off the road onto a soft shoulder and had whipped around in a full spin. Everybody else in the car was a nervous wreck but she had been calm throughout, calm until later when she had time to think about it. But now nothing had happened yet and already she was too frightened to catch her breath.

He said: "You are not leaving."

She couldn't say anything.

"You are not leaving," he repeated. "Women do not leave El Tigre until he has finished with them. Women do not walk out on El Tigre."

"Look—"

"Shut up."

The same level voice. The same vicious tone. She shut up.

"I am going to make love to you," he said. Except he didn't say "make love." He used another word that was four letters long and the way he said it made her feel filthy inside.

He said it again. Then he said the word itself several times, pronouncing it clearly and distinctly.

"There is nothing you can do," he said. "If you struggle with me I will hurt you and I will win anyway. If you scream no one will hear your cries. Frankly, I will be pleased if you fight because it will give me great pleasure to hurt you, and the more you fight the more I will hurt you and in the end it will be the same.

"I hope you struggle. You are a stupid *Norteamericana* bitch and your pain will give me considerable pleasure. I hope you scream because your screaming will be music to my ears, sweeter than the music that is playing over the stereo system. I will hurt you and I will make love to you and if you fight me hard enough I will kill you."

He was telling the truth. She stood there, unable to speak and unable to move, and she knew that every word he spoke was true. He would do as he said. If she fought him he would win, if she fought him hard enough he would kill her. He was not lying.

But this made no difference. She would have to fight him, even if it meant only pain for her, even if the outcome was no less certain. She would have to scream, even if the screams only added to his pleasure, even if no one but him ever heard her. She would claw and scream and struggle because she had no other choice.

"Take off your clothes."

"No."

Then he hit her.

It was a slap, not a punch. His open hand caught her across the face and she reeled. She started to fall—then he came around and hit her backhanded on the other side of her face and she straightened up again. Her face was red where he hit her and it hurt.

"Take off your clothes."

"No."

He opened the black silk robe and slipped it from his shoulders. He was naked.

He came closer. She tried to back away but she couldn't because of the bed. She held her breath because she knew what was coming. And then he hit her again.

Not a slap but a jab with the full force of his muscular body behind it.

Not in the face. In the stomach.

Then it began in earnest. He forced her down on the bed, tore at her clothing. She fought back, screaming, shrieking, tearing at him with her nails. She managed to rake the side of his cheek and he cursed in Spanish and released her.

But only for a moment. Then he sank his fist into her stomach and she cried out again in agony.

It went on. She fought with everything she had but it was somehow not enough. He was stronger, more determined, more experienced. He pounded her stomach until it ached incessantly, beat her in the breasts until they felt as though they were on fire. He drove one knee between her thighs and into her soft underbelly and she felt as though she was being ripped in half.

The beating did not stop. Even when she could resist him no more he didn't give up punishing her. He went on, hurting her, torturing her.

And then a very strange thing happened.

Very strange.

So strange she didn't understand it at first. So strange she couldn't think about it, couldn't even realize what it was. All she could do was react.

The fire in her breasts and loins turned from pain to pleasure.

The ache that dominated her entire being became an ache that craved immediate satisfaction. She didn't want to escape, not any more.

She wanted something else.

Something quite different.

Something she had never wanted before.

And she took what she wanted. She surprised him, her nails no longer reaching for his face but reaching instead for him, gripping his shoulders, pulling him down to her. Her mouth met his and they kissed but their type of lovemaking had little use for kisses.

Her thighs separated and he sank between them. His body pressed down against her and his hard chest hurt her poor breasts but she didn't mind the pain. Her legs wound around him and gripped him, drawing him to her, holding him tight and secure.

She began to move with him. Her movements were automatic now, unlike any time in the past. She didn't have to think what she was doing. She couldn't have thought about it if she had wanted to.

The music on the stereo system swelled up and around, louder and stronger. She didn't hear it. She heard nothing, nothing at all, because she could no longer hear.

She could not smell or hear or see or taste. She could only feel, feel the new and delicious and totally unfamiliar sensations that coursed through her lush body, could only feel him so hard and strong and cruel against her, could feel nothing but him inside her and herself around him.

It was not gentle lovemaking. It was not tenderness or kindness or sweetness.

It was anything but that.

It was hard and fast, vicious and violent, swift and relentless. It was harsh, wicked, sinful. It hurt but she didn't mind the hurt, pained but she didn't mind the pain, ached but the ache was sheer joy to her. Her body was alive for the first time and her veins and arteries sang with the physical beauty of it.

Faster.

Time stood still. Time, precisely, ceased to exist. The world fell away and the big round bed was a world in itself, a Paradise and a Hell at once, a fitful frenetic demanding pleasure pit.

Still faster.

She had never had a climax, never in her life, and when it started to happen she didn't recognize it for what it was. She held him in a death-grip and shrieked like a banshee, not sure whether she was dying or whether she was just beginning to live.

Her insides churned and her thighs around him were bands of molten lead. His teeth sank into her shoulder and she dug her nails deep into his back and neither of them noticed the pain. It was happening, it was happening, it was happening to her . . .

She reached orgasm at the precise moment that he did.

She collapsed.

Instantly she lost consciousness. She slept like a corpse, slept in the big round bed with him in her arms and her heart still pounding.

He got up.

Slowly, laboriously, George Sutton pulled himself to his feet. He was drained, physically and emotionally empty and exhausted.

For a moment he was unsteady on his feet and almost fell again to the padded floor of the compartment. Then he held his balance and took several deep breaths. It was an effort to breathe but it helped clear his head and he was steady again.

He dressed as quickly as he could. His hands were shaky and he put his underwear on inside-out at first, laughed self-consciously and got undressed and started over again. When he was fully dressed he got a cigarette going. He took several long drags on it and held the smoke in his lungs until it made him dizzy.

All this time Letitia remained where she was on the floor. Now, when he was fully dressed with a cigarette burning between his lips, she sprang lightly to her feet and slipped on her blue kimono. She seemed completely at ease, completely relaxed and well rested.

He didn't know how in the world she managed it and he couldn't help admiring her.

She flashed him a smile and turned to go. Something made him reach out a hand to stop her and she misinterpreted the gesture, removing her kimono and reaching out to embrace him. He smiled and shook his head and she raised her eyebrows, puzzled.

He reached out a hand, stroked her breasts once more. She looked at him and he let his hand drop and reached with his other hand for his wallet. There were still the two fives in his wallet and he gave one to the girl. Her eyes widened; then the smile spread on her face and she slipped the money into a God-given hiding place. George hoped they wouldn't search there for it.

She opened the door for him and they left. He followed her through the passageways until they somehow arrived in the room where they had started. The neat young man in the brown suit was waiting for them.

"Everything is all right?"

He nodded. Everything was all right.

"There is a car to return you to your hotel. Are you ready to leave?"

He nodded again.

"I am glad everything was to your liking. We shall be honored if you will return again."

George nodded again, almost curtly. He was tired and he wanted to get on his way. He didn't feel up to a conversation on the fine points of the show.

"Tell your friends about us," the neat young man said, and George got a hysterical picture of himself spreading the good word far and wide. He felt like laughing but he didn't have the strength.

The neat young man opened a door. George walked through it and another man held the door of a taxi for him. George sank into the back seat, mumbled his address and closed his eyes. He nearly fell asleep on the way back.

It had been an experience. That was an understatement—it had been an evening to end all evenings. The imagination and zeal of the performers was incredible—after the woman had had her turn with the girl, the short man took over for a round and the two of them went through some phenomenal paces.

Then the young girl gave up her pose of unwilling-partici-pant-in-obscene-games and became an equally zealous partner. With the three of them all going at once things got confusing, albeit exhilarating.

George shuddered. The complexity of situations with three participants was evidently endless. The short man, the soft young girl, the heavy-breasted woman—all three a tangle of arms and legs and breasts and bellies and sex organs, all three sweating and panting and moaning and biting and kissing and squirming...

Finally it had ended. Finally the lights went out on stage and he and Letitia were left alone.

And that was no bore, either.

The stimulation of the sex show had an unbelievable effect upon him. No amount of lovemaking seemed to tire him. He and Letitia went on for what seemed like eternity, duplicating items from the show and making up others, improvising on a theme ages old, moving together until they could move no more. If someone had told him that he was capable of that much lovemaking he wouldn't have believed it for a minute. But it had happened—over and over, again and again.

They crossed the border and arrived at the Plaza Hotel. George gave the driver his last five dollar bill, not caring that he was paying far more than was necessary, only wanting to get back to the room, to Mona. He had to see her; at the same time he dreaded seeing her. His emotions were so confused that he didn't even try to figure them out. He knew only that he had to get back to the room, to see her. That was all.

I must look like hell, he thought as he walked through the door and into the lobby. He glanced in the mirror and didn't know whether to grin wolfishly or to be sick to his stomach.

Mercifully neither the night clerk nor the elevator boy said a word. Mercifully he got to his floor without attracting any obvious attention. He walked quickly down the corridor to his room and knocked on the door.

There was no answer. He looked at his watch for the first time and found out to his surprise that it was after five. He hadn't even thought about the time, didn't think that it was later or earlier than what it was. It was as if time had been suspended from the moment he had met Ernesto.

She must be sleeping, he thought. He turned his key in the lock and pushed the door open.

The room was empty.

He looked in the bathroom, even peered into the closet and, for some unknown reason, took a quick glance under the bed.

No Mona.

He shook his head, wondering where she was, worrying about her, worrying about himself, wondering what in God's name had happened to her. He checked the drawers to see if she had packed and run out on him but all her clothes were where she had left them.

Where in hell—

He called the lobby; nobody had seen her all night long. He thought of calling the police and decided against it. Wearily he sat down on the edge of the bed to wait for her.

He was tired, so tired. After a few minutes he stretched out on the bed with his head on the pillow. He didn't bother to get undressed because he didn't plan on sleeping.

He didn't plan on closing his eyes either but they closed by themselves. His mind blurred and his head swam.

Seconds later he was asleep.

CHAPTER 5

She wasn't sure how she felt.

El Tigre had called a cab for her. When El Tigre wanted something it came to him in short order, whether it was a cab or a woman, and the taxi arrived in front of his house in no time at all. El Tigre talked to the driver and passed him a bill, paying her cab fare. Now she was sitting in the back seat by herself while the cab, a broken-down Pontiac coupe that must have been the half-hearted survivor of untold accidents, headed toward the bridge, the United States, the city of Laredo and, to be specific, the Plaza Hotel.

And she, in the back seat, was Mona.

Mona Sutton.

Wife of George Sutton.

Mistress of El Tigre.

Whore of Babylon.

And, naturally, she didn't know how she felt.

The rays of the sun were warm on the side of her neck through the dirty window of the taxi and she glanced at her watch to find out just how late it was. It was, she discovered, pretty darned late—8:30 by her watch, and her watch was never more than a few minutes off one way or the other. She stared fixedly at her watch, marveling at what a miraculous mechanism it was to keep such fine time for her.

It was a gold watch with a plain black suede band and she thought that it was the perfect sort of watch for her, dressy while still simple, attractive without being flashy in any way. She went on staring at the watch, mainly to avoid thinking about anything more disturbing than watches and time, and she remembered that George had given it to her on their second anniversary.

Which got her thinking of George.

She felt guilty, inevitably. But more disturbing than the guilt was the notion in the back of her mind that she was feeling guilty for the wrong thing. Her infidelity itself didn't bother her. She had been unfaithful before; she had already expected to be unfaithful sometime in the future. Fidelity, as far as she was concerned, was a word, an abstract noun to be used in the titles of insurance companies and very little more. If two people were married and in love with each other, an occasional sampling by one party of the sexual proficiency or lack of it of a third party shouldn't be something to make God frown too terribly.

Besides, she added mentally, it wasn't as if she had flown about looking to get herself rolled in the hay. It wasn't that way at all. George had gone off to his hot little sideshow with a hot little Mexican to keep him company and she had been justifiably depressed. Her state of depression had led her to drink, one drink had led to another, and before she knew quite what was happening she was in a bedroom with a lecherous sadist.

So it was hardly her fault.

Not her fault at all. Why, once she was sober enough to realize what the man was planning she did her damnedest to get out of the place. He was too strong for her—the whole thing had been rape pure and simple; since when did a woman have to feel guilty of being the victim of a rape? That was a new one.

She got out a cigarette, got it going and took a deep drag on it. It didn't taste very good but it gave her something to do. Then she had to roll down the window to throw away the match and that gave her something else to do. After another drag she decided that she didn't like the cigarette at all, and that gave her still another thing to do. She threw it out of the window.

But then she didn't have anything more to do outside of lighting another cigarette and she really didn't want another cigarette. She wanted one even less than she had wanted the first one, which was very little indeed. And she decided that it wasn't worth going through the process of lighting another cigarette just so she wouldn't have to admit what she really felt guilty about.

So what the hell.

Why not admit it?

She felt guilty because she had enjoyed it to the hilt, enjoyed the beating and the horrible lovemaking, enjoyed it afterwards when she had held him in her arms and listened while he said things to her in Spanish which she did not understand. She enjoyed it the second time he made love to her, still with a special sort of the violence which was evidently characteristic of his lovemaking but more gently.

She had enjoyed it.

Hell.

Enjoyed it?

She loved every bloody minute of it.

She took a deep breath, let it out slowly and tried to relax.

They were crossing the border now—the cab was on the bridge and in a minute they would be about to enter the United States, the state of Texas, the city of Laredo. Back home back to sanity, back to safety and security and, of course, back to George.

Back to monotony.

Safe monotony, to be sure. Secure monotony, monotony that would never kill her or maim her or break her sweet little heart.

But no less monotonous as a result.

She lowered her head as they passed over the border and gazed at her body. Gingerly she cupped her full breasts with her hands, squeezing them but squeezing them as gently as she possibly could. They still ached from the beating he had given her and she couldn't touch herself there without a spurt of pain, without her body stiffening perceptibly and her flesh crying out.

Pain or no pain, she squeezed them again. She liked the pain. She liked the memory of how he had hurt her breasts, of the arrogant way in which he had abused her, of his lips and tongue when he kissed her breasts afterward.

She let go of her breasts and slipped one hand under her skirt. She ran the hand up between her thighs and touched herself, just as she had touched herself before in the bar while she was in the process of getting stinking drunk.

Now it was different.

For one thing, she hadn't ached there before. Now she hurt terribly.

For another thing, a more important thing, she hadn't been alive there before. It seemed almost as if that part of her anatomy was an electrical appliance that she had always carried around with her but had never plugged in. Now, now that El Tigre had activated the electrical current, the appliance was useful for the first time.

Very useful.

Eminently useful.

Inordinately useful.

But where she wondered, did she go from here?

The answer, incomplete and unsatisfactory, came almost at once. The cab driver pulled the car to a sudden stop in front of the Plaza Hotel as if he had just read her mind and she pitched forward, catching herself just before she would have rammed into the front seat. She straightened up and managed to get out of the cab.

The answer was obvious.

From here she went upstairs to her room. To George.

To monotony.

Then they would get out of town as soon as the two of them had had a decent night's sleep. Or a decent day's sleep, since it was close to nine now and you could hardly call it the night any more. The night was over and done with, and it had surely been one hell of a night.

Yes, they would get out of town. They could go to Mexico City, either to continue their vacant vacation or to get the quickie divorce that was in the back of both of their minds. Or, possibly, they could get to hell and gone away from Mexico. If they needed a divorce she could pick one up in Reno; after George's trip to the sex show and her participation in her own private sex show, Mexico might well have lost a good deal of its charm. If nothing else, the rest of the country might prove anticlimactic.

The last word in her train of thought was, she decided, a good pun. She laughed shortly.

Yes, they'd have to get out of Nueva Laredo. Another meeting with El Tigre might be fun but it might also be fatal. The best thing that could happen to her now would be to settle down with George. True, the pair of them would never set any records between the sheets—but they loved each other and they gave each other a good feeling of essential and warm security. A good home and a good husband did not grow on the nearest bush.

She walked into the hotel. The key wasn't at the desk and she guessed that George had gone upstairs. It seemed like a fairly safe guess. She took the elevator to her floor and walked to her door, unsure whether she ought to knock or not. He was probably sleeping and he might not be too delighted with the idea of being awakened.

She knocked once softly. Nothing happened. Then she knocked a second time, louder, and again nothing happened. Either George was dead to the world or he was just plain dead. And she didn't much care which.

She walked back down the corridor, rang for the elevator and rode it to the main floor. The desk clerk managed to come up with a pass key after hunting around in the drawer for what seemed like hours. He rode up with her a second time in the elevator and led her back to the room.

He opened the door, craning his neck in order to get a look at the inside of the room. She managed to turn her body so as to maneuver him out of the way, then smiled sweetly at him and slipped through the door, shutting it behind her.

George was, as she had guessed, either dead to the world or

just plain dead. She stood at the foot of the bed and looked down on him, stared hard at his face and thought about him and about herself.

She tried to picture herself doing the things with George that she had done with El Tigre. She tried to imagine him exciting her, hurting her, driving her so insane that she no longer knew what she was doing or even cared about it. She went through the whole scene with El Tigre in her mind only this time El Tigre had George's face and George's body.

It was a good-looking face and a good-looking body. George was by no means an unattractive man. Now, when he was asleep with his body all sprawled out and his face untroubled, he looked younger than he was, younger and more appealing. His face had character and strength—not the hard brutality of El Tigre, not the force and ferocity of the Mexican, but a charm that was hardly unattractive.

George was appealing.

But not to her.

And the mental picture, the whole mental filmstrip that was rolling through her brain, the impossible image of herself and George in a sexual death grip, was unreal and absurd and almost offensive.

She turned away from the bed and took a few steps toward the bathroom, then wheeled around and paced methodically and aimlessly toward the bed once again. Her clothing was like a straightjacket and she fought her way out of it, hanging it over the back of a chair. She stripped all the way down until she was completely naked and stood in the middle of the floor examining her body for bruises.

There were plenty of them. She had taken one hell of a beating, all things taken into consideration. One grand hell of a beating.

And just thinking about it was exciting.

She started to pace the floor again but she didn't want to walk around naked. She didn't feel right that way and she had to stop after a few steps and sit down on the edge of the bed. She planted her feet on the floor and cupped her hands over her knees so that the inside edge of each arm pressed against one of her breasts.

She was tired, physically and emotionally and mentally tired, but she didn't want to go to sleep and she had a feeling she wouldn't be able to sleep. She was almost too tired to sleep, if such a state existed, and all she wanted to do was to lie or sit somewhere without moving a muscle or thinking about anything at all.

She turned, ready to lie down on the bed next to George, but before she could do it something indefinable made her turn again and stand up on her feet. She didn't know what was causing it but she couldn't even lie next to George, couldn't bear to lie with him or sleep with him or anything.

And, suddenly, she knew that the decision she had made in the cab was a decision that she could never go through with. A life with George, a life of Connecticut boredom and sexless apathy, might be the better life for her. If that night hadn't happened, if they had never come to Mexico in the first place, if Nueva Laredo was just a spot on the map, if . . .

There were a lot of *ifs*. But what it spelled out was quite simple: after what had happened for her that night, for her and to her, she could never be content with what had gone before. After a night with El Tigre she could never live through another night with George. After a night of passion she couldn't conceivably endure a night of nothingness.

You can't go home again, she thought. It would be like trying to grow her hymen back again, trying to recover a mental maidenhead which had been torn to ribbons that night.

It would never work.

Never.

She made another picture. The picture was set in Connecticut, in a little house complete with an Oldsmobile in the driveway and a television set in the living room. There was the standard allotment of three children raising mild hell throughout the house, the standard invitations to the standard parties, the standard sheaf of bills and ads that had come in the morning's mail. There was a pile of dishes to be placed in the automatic dishwasher, a chuteful of laundry to be stuffed into the washing machine, a list of groceries to be ordered from the A&P.

She tried to put herself into the picture. It was like the ads—*Put yourself into this picture.*

But she couldn't.

She didn't fit any more.

She sat down heavily in a chair, crossed her legs and folded her arms. She thought instead about the other course of life open to her, the life that seemed to be the only one she could select.

It was, all in all, one hell of a life.

Life with El Tigre. Life as his mistress, doing what he told her, taking his abuse and cherishing it, living in sickness and depravity and perversion.

It was quite a picture.

One hell of a picture. One hell of a damnably unpleasant

picture, a picture she didn't like in the least. But there was one disturbing thing about it.

This picture fit her like a diaphragm. In this picture she matched the furniture and her dress didn't clash with the wallpaper. In this picture she was completely at home.

She swallowed.

She tried to relax in the chair but she couldn't. She couldn't move at all any longer and all she could do was remain in the chair, motionless and unseeing, her legs crossed and her arms folded across her breasts. After awhile her eyes closed and her breathing regulated itself and she looked as though she was sleeping.

She wasn't.

When he woke up, even before his eyes were opened, he felt foul and filthy and sick. He wanted to rip off his head and stuff it between the mattress and the spring. He wanted to wash himself inside and out with scalding water mixed fifty-fifty with rubbing alcohol.

He did neither of these things. Instead he opened his eyes and tried to see through them. It wasn't easy but he managed it.

The first and only thing he saw was his wife sitting in the chair with no clothes on, her eyes shut and her legs crossed and her arms folded across her breasts. It took him a good ten seconds to realize who she was, that it was his wife, that it was Mona, that he was in a hotel room in Laredo looking at his naked wife.

Well, he thought dully, this is a new one. You live year after year and you play everything according to the rules and you figure you have enough experience so that you know how to react to just about any situation. Then one afternoon you wake up in a bed in a hotel room in Laredo looking at your naked wife who is sitting in a chair with her arms folded over her breasts and her legs crossed. You've spent the past night at a sex show and God alone can say where she's been.

Now, you son of a bitch, what do you do now?

He tossed a few possible courses of action around in his head, launched a few ideas to see if any of them orbited, and finally said something which was not particularly brilliant, in addition to being inaccurate. He said: "Good morning." Since it was neither good nor morning it didn't seem especially well chosen for the occasion but he didn't care too much about it any more.

She didn't answer.

"Hell," he said. He reached up one hand and scratched his head, pondering.

"Lousy afternoon," he said this time.

Her eyes opened.

This time he couldn't think of a thing to say. "Where were you all night?" he managed.

Her eyes closed again, remained closed for nearly a full minute, and then opened once more.

"Out."

"That much I knew. I thought maybe—"

Her eyes closed.

"Well?"

With her eyes still closed she said: "How about you? Did you enjoy the sex show?"

"Very much."

"See anything exciting? Get all hot and bothered by it?"

He didn't answer.

"What did you do—masturbate? That must have been fun. You're a real man, George."

He sat up in bed, reached for cigarettes and got one going. He still didn't say anything.

"Pardon me," she said. "I don't want to cast aspersions on your manhood. You probably didn't have to do the job yourself anyway. You had a girl with you, didn't you?"

After a moment he said that he had.

"What was she like?"

He shrugged automatically. Then he realized that she couldn't see the shrug with her eyes closed and he said: "She was all right."

"Did she do what you wanted her to do?"

"Yes."

"And did you both have a good time?"

He took a deep drag on the cigarette and coughed. The bitch, he thought. The miserable bitch.

He said: "She gave me a damned better lay than you ever did, Mona."

"Really?"

"Really."

"You must be hot stuff," she said, and he saw that she was smiling. "You must be pretty good to get her so excited. Of course the money you paid her couldn't have had anything to do with her interest, could it?"

"Mona—"

She laughed. "Why don't you tell me about it, George? Tell me what you did and what you saw. Tell me everything, my sweet husband."

He looked at her, thinking that this naked female couldn't

be his wife, thinking that somehow she was completely different than she had ever been before, that there was nothing about her that excited him or interested him, nothing that could possibly motivate him to love her.

How had he ever been in love with her? How could the frigid bitch get him so damned upset? He looked her over from feet to hair, looked at her breasts and her hips, looked at her and saw her not as a desirable woman but as a cold piece of naked and not-too-attractive flesh.

To hell with her.

"Sure," he said. "I'll tell you."

"Will you?"

That damned smile.

"If you want."

"I'd like to hear. I might learn something."

"Not you—you never learn."

"You think I'm too old to learn?"

"Too cold to learn's more like it. You can't teach a cold bitch new tricks."

The smile again. "Tell me, George."

And he told her. He gave her the whole story from beginning to end, told her about the heavy-breasted woman and the small man and the soft young girl, told her everything they did and the sounds they made while they were doing it and the expressions on their faces. He didn't tell it clinically. He used the four-letter words and the five-letter words, the words men scrawled on public lavatory walls and the words kids chalked on the sidewalks. He gave her a fitting and precise summary of everything that happened on stage and everything that took place in his own compartment, told her about Letitia and the sexy little tricks the Mexican girl knew, told her about every gesture and every caress and every moan.

All the while she didn't open her eyes, didn't speak, didn't uncross her legs or unfold her arms from around her big breasts.

And all the while the strange and unfamiliar smile never left her face.

"Are you finished? "

"I'm finished."

"That's all you did?"

"Isn't it enough?" It was his turn to smile.

"Maybe," she said. "Maybe it's enough."

He lit another cigarette.

"Don't you want to hear about my evening?"

He shrugged again, realized again that her eyes were still closed, and told her aloud that he frankly didn't give a good goddamn.

"Of course," she said, "compared to your evening, mine was fairly routine."

"It was?"

"Certainly," she said. "But you might as well hear about it. You might even be a little surprised."

"Think so?" He didn't really care. He just wanted her to shut up and leave him alone.

Her eyes opened. "I think so."

"Then go ahead and tell me."

She unfolded her arms, uncrossed her legs. Then the smile widened and a crazy gleam came into her eyes and she opened her mouth to laugh out loud. He stared at her and didn't know what to make of it.

"I'll tell you, George."

She cupped her full breasts with her hands. Then as he watched she moved her thighs and stroked herself with one finger. She winked at him and the wink was obscene.

"My man," she said. "My big strong sexy lover of a husband. My George."

He held his breath.

"George wants to hear," she said, half to herself and half to him. "Big George wants to hear the whole stimulating story from beginning to end. Well, George will hear. All George has to do is listen carefully and he'll hear every bit of the story. Every last word, just like George told me. George is a good husband and he has a perfect right to know."

She fondled herself with her finger, massaging her breasts with her other hand as she did so. Her breasts were a glowing pink and there was color in her face. He wondered if she was going insane, if some little wheel had slipped within her brain. He almost felt like calling a doctor but he couldn't even manage to reach for the phone to place a call. He was too entranced, too wrapped up in some awful morbid fascination to move or speak or even breathe easily.

She raised her finger to her lips and kissed it greedily. Then she put it where it had been and stroked herself rhythmically. As she stroked herself she began to speak and her words came out in a rhythm that matched that of her finger.

"Poor little George," she was saying. "Poor little George who gets his kicks watching. Poor little George who can't get his wife hot to trot. Poor little George."

Talking and probing, talking and stroking, her whole body beginning to take up the rhythm.

"George likes to look," she said. "Maybe George likes to listen too. You like to listen, Georgie? You get hot listening? You ever listen to those dirty records they've got of men and women doing it?"

He said nothing.

Her eyes shone. "You can look and listen, Georgie. You can watch me while I play and you can listen to me while I tell you. Listen carefully, Georgie. Listen real carefully."

CHAPTER 6

There are bars in Laredo. There are bars across the border on the Mexican side as well, but there is a difference between the American bars and the Mexican bars, just as there is a similar difference between Mexican bars catering to the tourist trade and Mexican bars catering to Mexicans.

The Laredo bars sell rye and bourbon and Scotch. They also sell beer, of course, as well as rum and vodka and gin. But rum and vodka and gin are dirt cheap on the other side of the border and the rum-drinkers and vodka-drinkers and gin-drinkers generally take their trade across the Rio Grande. If you are a rum-drinker or a vodka-drinker or a gin-drinker, it makes good sense to pay the five cents, walk across the border, take a skinful and pay another nickel to walk back across the bridge. There's no import duty on liquor if you bring it in inside you.

If you are a don't-care drinker you pick the bar you like and sit there. If you are the roaming type of drinker you start at one end of the social scale and move on down the line, with a drink here and two drinks there and so on until you are blotto enough so that you don't know or care where you are. You start in Laredo on Scotch, cross over to a tourist bar and drink rum, and wind up throwing hot shots of tequila down your already anesthetized throat in one of the native establishments where nobody gives a damn how drunk you get.

George Sutton started in a Laredo bar. To be precise, he started in the bar downstairs at the Plaza Hotel, but the two drinks he had there didn't really count. It was around the corner at the Silver Fox Bar and Grill that things began to move.

He threw the two double shots of rye down his throat without tasting them, signaled for a third double and put it the same place he had put the first two. He looked at his watch, more from force of habit than from any genuine desire to discover what time it was, and found out that it was almost seven in the evening.

The night was young. Here he was, a free man spending a night on the town, and the night was young. What could be nicer than that?

As he was drinking the next drink he remembered it all, the scene in the hotel room, the words Mona had spoken and the pictures they conjured up in his brain. He remembered it all and he knew that now it was over, over forever, that he and Mona were wrong for each other to begin with and that even if they weren't it was over. Over completely, because two people couldn't go through a scene like that one and ever want to see each other again.

So here he was having a night on the town. He had a very large capacity for liquor, a capacity that even another ad man might envy, and his head was still relatively clear. In time his brain would start to swim a bit, and if he tied one on firmly enough he would undoubtedly black out and do things that he would fail to remember afterwards. Then, eventually, he would pass out somewhere and sleep anywhere from five to ten hours, depending primarily upon where he was when he passed out and how long he had been drinking before it happened.

Some men, when they drink, get drunk without planning to. Others are careful to keep on the thin line that divides highness from drunkenness. Others are gone from the minute they take the first drink. George Sutton was another type altogether. He was drinking to get drunk, and he knew that he would become completely drunk, do things he wouldn't otherwise do and be sorry afterward that he hadn't stayed sober. He realized all of this in advance and he went ahead anyway.

What the hell difference did it make?

Besides, and more important, he *wanted* to get drunk. It was something that he wanted, really wanted, wanted with every last stinking fiber of his stinking being. And there were not many things in the world he wanted.

In fact, all things considered, there wasn't a single stinking thing in the whole stinking world that he really and truly deep down inside him wanted.

Except, of course, to get drunk.

He didn't want Mona. Hell, he never wanted to see her again. He couldn't even hate her; all he could do was think what a huge mistake the whole affair had been. For him she had been frigid—for another man she had turned into a forest fire. A forest fire—and he imagined what she would be like on fire, burning with a bright passionate flame, and his hand was shaking when he took the next drink.

To hell with Mona. He didn't even want to kill her, which was supposed to be the natural reaction under such conditions. He had no feeling toward her at all except an overwhelming ache in the pit of his gut over the mess he had made out of everything, over the hellish turn things had taken. That was all—a dull dead pain that the alcohol would in time soothe.

But what, outside of getting drunk, did he want?

He could go back to New York, sell the house in Connecticut and get a Manhattan apartment and a good mistress. But he didn't even want the mistress. And the thought of working again in the ad agency, dreaming up new and improved ways to sell new and improved soap, futzing around with cabs and subways and theatre tickets and waiters . . .

No. He did not want to go back to New York.

To hell with New York, he decided. What was the matter with Laredo? Nice town, Laredo. Nice place to live. Friendly town filled to overflowing with friendly people. A nice place to hang your hat.

Laredo.

Garden spot of Southeast Texas.

Gateway to Mexico.

Whorehouse to the western world.

So why not remain in Laredo?

Well, there were several good reasons. Number One seemed to be money. How would he make a living in Laredo? Conceivably they needed ad men in Laredo as well as in Ulcer Gulch, although why they needed ad men *anywhere* was a tough question for him to answer at the moment. Still, with the experience he had under his belt he shouldn't have any trouble convincing the local yokels to give him a nice cushy job. Of course he wouldn't take home the kind of money he took home in the big city, but he didn't need that kind of money any more.

There was really only one drawback to the notion. It entailed working and he didn't want to do any more work. He wanted to retire.

Now that would be a good move. Retiring at his age—that would be a positive joy to contemplate. The only rough spot was that you needed money to retire, money or a pension or coupons to clip or something.

And, with all the traveler's checks he had cashed and all the money in the room, he had a grand total of seven hundred odd dollars.

Which wouldn't go too far.

In fact, he mused, it wasn't altogether out of the realm of possibility that the seven hundred would be gone before the night was over.

He laughed to himself. He could always sell the car, could always wire home and have the house sold, could always raise enough money to keep himself alive. That was all that mattered. There was nothing he wanted, nothing he needed, and as a result there was no longer any way in which he could be hurt. They couldn't hurt him any more. You couldn't hurt a man who didn't have a desire in the world. All that could happen to him was that he could die, and he didn't even want to go on living.

He was, for the first time in his life, one hundred percent safe.

One hundred percent free.

Free. He thought of the Four Freedoms and realized with something approaching happiness that he had them all. Freedom from want, to begin with, and even though he couldn't recall the other three at the moment the one took care of the others.

So he was free.

So free that he didn't have to stay in that particular bar another minute. He got up, left a tip for the bartender and got the hell out of the bar. It was a cool night and a clear night and it was only a short walk to the bridge. His legs were sturdy and his stride was easy and he made it to the bridge in no time. He wasn't even breathing hard when he hit the other side.

"You got a match?"

The girl who asked the question was a nicely stacked redhead who was about thirty years old and well on the way to public intoxication. A limp unlighted cigarette dangled from a pair of full red lips and a pack of matches at her elbow indicated that she didn't really need a match at all. This hint wasn't necessary; the look in her eyes told him the same thing.

He lit her cigarette and ordered a pair of drinks for the two of them.

"What's your name?"

"Sutton," he told her. And at the precise moment in time he stopped being George and became Sutton. George was a nobody who sold advertising; Sutton was a nobody who drank and wasted his time in Mex bars. George didn't exist any more. He stopped existing right then and there at 9:10 of a Thursday night and Sutton replaced him.

"Sutton," the redhead said. "Like Willy Sutton?"

He shrugged.

She sipped her drink—she was drinking grasshoppers, which always struck Sutton as a particularly noxious way to get loaded—and she smiled up at him.

"I'm Marie Wilks, Sutton. You can call me Marie if you want. Or if you'd rather you can call me Wilks."

He nodded.

"You don't look happy," she said, pursing her lips. "Whatsa matter?"

"Nothing."

"You happy?"

"No."

"You sad?"

"No."

"Just blah, huh? You just feel sort of blah, Sutton? Is that it?"

"Yeah," he said. "That's about it."

"You like me?"

He just looked at her.

"You think I'm pretty?"

He looked at her again and a smile spread on his face. "Stand up," he told her.

She stood up.

"Now turn around. That's right. Stick out your tits a little. Shake your rear. Lift your skirt a little so I can get a look at your legs. Okay, sit down now."

When she was seated on the stool again he said: "Yeah, you're pretty. You got a good head of hair and a good pair of knockers and a nice round butt and a pretty face. You're okay."

"Thanks."

"Is all of it yours?"

"I dyed the hair," she said. "It used to be the color of mud."

"Are the tits yours?"

"Feel 'em and find out."

He grinned, then reached out with one hand and took hold of her breast. She was wearing a sweater, a black cashmere sweater, and there was nothing under it but her. He took a long time handling her and she was smiling too by the time he let go of her.

"All me," she said.

"Firm," he said. "Nice firm meat."

"You didn't try the other one."

"No need to."

"Wouldn't you like to?"

"Want me to?"

"Sure, Sutton. You got nice hands. I like the touch of hands to make me feel young again."

He touched her again.

"Let's go sit in the booth," she suggested. "Let's go in back and sit in one of the booths and have a few more drinks, Sutton."

"So we can touch each other some more?"

"So every bastard in creation can't watch us."

"Let them watch," he said. "I don't give a damn."

"*I* do."

He shrugged again because he didn't really care one way or the other. He got up from the stool and let her lead him to a booth near the back of the bar. He sat down first and then she sat down on the seat next to him and put her feet up on the seats across from them. She put one hand on his leg and gave him a little squeeze.

"Do you like me, Sutton?"

"Sure," he said, wondering idly what she would say if he told her he hated her. No point in saying that, he decided. She was a nice enough dame and he *did* like her, as far as it went. They'd wind up going to bed somewhere if they stayed sober enough, and the way she was built it ought to be fun.

"What do you like about me?"

"Your tits."

"Is that all?"

"That's all I've had a hand on so far."

"Why don't you find out if there isn't something else about me you like?"

He put one hand under her skirt and ran it upwards along the inside of her leg all the way to the top. He kept his hand there a long time, touching her.

"Okay," he said. "I like that part too."

"That's my personality."

"Huh?"

"I had a face full of pimples when I was a kid," she explained. "You can have the nicest bosom in creation but if you've got a face full of acne you don't get too many dates. Not unless you have something else. Like a lot of personality."

He didn't say anything.

"I had personality," she went on. "I had as many dates as I wanted because all of the boys liked my personality. We would park somewhere and neck each other up and then I'd lift my skirt and there was my personality. That's what I call it."

"You've got a nice personality."

"You're okay, Sutton."

"Thanks."

"You just don't give a damn, huh? I could sit here and tell you the story of my life and you just wouldn't give a damn. I could cry my eyes out and you wouldn't bat a pubic hair. Right?"

"Right."

"Then buy me another drink."

He ordered another round. They both drank them quickly and she said: "Wanta get loved, Sutton?"

He didn't answer.

"I'm not gonna bother being cute about it," she said. "You might say I'm past the point of subtlety. I guess you might say that if you wanted to. All I know is that I've been had so many times that I don't have to play games any more. You know something, Sutton?"

"What?"

"I like being had. I like it, Sutton. You ever been married, Sutton?"

"I'm married now."

"You working at it?"

"Not any more."

"I'm divorced," she said. "Before I was married I ran around like a bitch in heat and I bedded anybody who wanted me. Damn near anybody, anyway. Then this guy came in from out of the blue and fell in love with me and I fell in love with him and it was like everything was roses. You know what I'm talking about?"

He nodded.

Marie said: "And he wanted to marry me. He didn't care about all the guys who went to the well before him. All he wanted was me and all I wanted was him and we got married. You ever been to Chicago, Sutton?"

"Couple of times."

"That's where we were. Chicago. Little house and he had a job in a factory. Skilled worker—tool and die man. I never did get straight on what the hell he did exactly at the plant but he brought home good money. We were in love with each other and it was roses."

He nodded again.

"Then one day this guy put the make on me and I got all hot and I let him. Frank didn't find out about it but it happened and *I* knew about it, so that was bad. You know what I mean? I was trying to stay clean for Frank and even if he didn't find out it was like I was dirty inside."

"Yeah."

"So after that it kept happening. I laid the mailman in the front hall and the doctor when he was examining me to find out if I was pregnant, which as it turned out I wasn't, and I slept with everybody else who ever walked within sleeping distance, and finally Frank found out and the marriage went blooey. So you won't be crawling into the hay with a virgin, Sutton."

"I don't like virgins."

"But if you want me, just say the word."

She put her hand on his leg again. He felt himself getting excited and she smiled because she could tell that he was getting excited.

"I'll be a good one," Marie said. "I'm always good. I really put my heart into it. Along with everything else."

He pushed her hand away. He took her arms and drew her out of the booth. "C'mon," he said harshly. "Let's go someplace."

"I'm glad you see it my way."

Outside he said: "I've got an idea. You ever been to a sex show?"

"Like where they have a Shetland pony humping a woman and things like that?"

"Like that. The one I'm thinking of has two girls and a guy. Ever been to one of those?"

"Never."

"Like to go?"

"What do you do there?"

"First you watch and then you use your own imagination."

"Is it good?"

He nodded.

"What the hell," she announced. "I'm twenty-nine years old and I've been loving like a goddamned rabbit for fourteen years. I'll try anything."

She took his arm and they walked off toward the Plaza. He was feeling the liquor but he walked steadily and he could still think straight. The only point he didn't feel sure of was the precise location of the sex show.

But that didn't matter.

Ernesto would know. Ernesto was a friend in need, and Ernesto would know.

Ernesto *did* know. It took a long time to find Ernesto but they found him and Ernesto was most obliging. Yes, he would take the *señor* and the *señorita* to the show. Yes, they would get there in time to see a complete show. No, the show was not the same every night. Tonight, for example, there would be different performers than last night.

Who would there be? Ernesto thought for a moment. Well, there would be a very attractive Negro girl who used a small dog in her act. Did the señor and the señorita think that would be amusing?

The señor thought it would be most amusing.

So did the señorita.

There would also be two men who would do things to the Negro girl. Did the señor and the señorita think that also would be amusing?

The señor thought it would be amusing.

The señorita concurred.

Then a white girl would join the party and the four of them would do things to each other—the two men and the Negro girl and the white girl. Did the señor and the señorita feel that such a display might be amusing as well?

The señor thought so.

The señorita agreed.

The price, however, would be higher. The show would last somewhat longer than the previous night's entertainment and there were, of course, more performers. Two more performers, if one counted the dog. And one had to count the dog because the dog behaved in a most amusing fashion.

How much higher?

Two hundred dollars.

Was that too expensive?

No, said the señor. That was not too expensive.

Then were the señor and the señorita ready to go?

The señor was ready to go.

So was the señorita.

They were so ready to go that they felt like making love in the street.

Chapter 7

Mona was in bed.

This in itself was hardly unusual. Mona was in bed most of the time nowadays, and in a sense the amount of time she spent in bed was singularly symbolic. She had made her bed and now she was lying in it.

It had been a little more than a week since she had left George, a little more than a week since she had moved in with El Tigre on a more or less permanent basis. As far as she was concerned it was permanent—she never wanted to leave him, never, no matter what he did with her. But she couldn't think of the relationship as something that would endure. Sooner or later he would tire of her; sooner or later he would kick her out on her tail with all due ceremony and she would have to find another place to hang her garter belt.

A little more than a week. Just how many days they had been living together was something she wasn't sure of. Living with El Tigre she lost all track of the time. One day followed another, and while one day might be a good day and another a bad day, and while all of the days were memorable and vital in some form or another, the days themselves were single units and time in the abstract was an impossible concept to keep hold of. She was alive, she was with El Tigre, and that was about all she was entirely certain about.

There was a certain routine about the days and nights. She had a room to herself and a bed to herself—not the bedroom in which he had first made love to her, not the huge circular bed, for that bed and that room were reserved for seductions. She had a small room with a three-quarter bed and a mahogany dresser. The carpeting covered the entire floor and was thick and luxurious, a deep wine-red carpet that added a delicate note of opulent sin to the room. Those were the only furnishings, the bed and the dresser. There was also a picture over the bed, a powerful Orozco with slashing lines to it, a picture of a group of workers working, she had decided, and since she didn't know the title of it she called it Workers Working to herself.

She slept in her room, in the bed which she was occupying at the moment. When she was not sleeping she was still in the room unless she was eating a meal or unless El Tigre wanted her. When El Tigre wanted her she went to him and did whatever he wished.

She had learned early that he was a satyr, a man with an almost unquenchable appetite for female flesh. Satyriasis, while never earning the contempt reserved for nymphomania, was much the same thing. No one woman could satisfy him. He had to have different women all the time, had to leave her bed for the bed of another woman.

In another man she would have despised this. But with El Tigre she did not despise it at all. It was, she told herself simply, just the way he was. She accepted it—just as she accepted everything he did and everything that he forced her to do. He made her do many things, many things that filled her with revulsion at first and some that she never managed to enjoy at all. There was one time when he made her perform an act which no amount of rationalization could lead her to accept as natural. It was perversion, plain and simple—rank vile perversion that not only hurt her so horribly that she felt herself wishing for death but also sickened her and nauseated her so that as soon as it was over she ran for a basin and her poor stomach turned inside-out.

He asked her to do the same thing the next night.

She didn't enjoy it this time, either. Again she was sick, again she was hurt horribly, again her whole body ached for the remainder of the evening.

And again she had done it willingly as she knew she would do absolutely anything that he might ask her to do.

She rearranged her position in the bed, snuggling her cheek against the pillow and arranging her hair so that it spread itself out over the pillow like a golden pillow slip. Air-conditioning kept the room nicely cold at night and the heavy blankets kept her warm in the cold room. She yawned deeply, then wriggled around again and sat upright in the bed, propping the pillow up against the headboard and leaning against it. She fumbled for the first cigarette of the day—there was no night table beside the bed but she had left a pack of cigarettes and a match on the floor at the side of the bed and she got one between her lips and lit it. It was a Mexican cigarette and not so tightly packed as the brand she had smoked in the United States but in the past week or so she had gotten used to it and now liked it as well as American cigarettes. The smoke tasted good in her lungs that morning and she smoked steadily, flicking her ashes in the ashtray that she also kept by the side of the bed and stubbing the cigarette out in the ashtray when she had finished it.

It was, she decided, a strange life. It was hard for her to believe now that she had ever been a run-of-the-mill suburban housewife, almost as impossible as it was to believe that she had ever been frigid. If anyone had told her a year ago that she would wind up as the passionate mistress of a perverted Mexican criminal she would have laughed aloud. But it had happened and she didn't know whether to laugh or to cry. Sometimes she felt like laughing, sometimes like crying, and sometimes she had no feelings at all. At those times she knew only that she had found her place, for better or for worse, and that her own personal happiness or sadness had nothing to do with it. She was beginning to discover that finding one's proper role was infinitely more important than one's state of mind, than happiness or sadness.

After she had finished the cigarette she sat in bed for a few moments thinking. Then she pushed back the bedcovers in one motion and hopped out of bed. She was hungry, very hungry all at once, and she slipped a robe over her bare body and put on a pair of deerskin bedroom slippers that El Tigre had given her. She washed and brushed her teeth, flashing a quick smile at the mirror. When she got downstairs the table in the breakfast nook was set for her and there was a glass of some sort of fruit juice at her place. She drank it; then Pandora appeared as silently as ever with a plateful of *huevos rancheros*—eggs ranch-style, which she had christened eggs raunch-style, three scrambled eggs with red pepper and green pepper and assorted spices that she preferred not to think about too carefully. The eggs were good as long as you didn't pay too much mind to what might be used in their preparation and she wolfed them down hungrily. Cafe con leche came next, bitter coffee cut with a lot of milk and made edible "or drinkable," to be precise by the addition of a boatload of sugar. She had a second cigarette with the coffee and she felt good by the time she was ready to leave the table.

The rest of the morning as well as the afternoon were spent in the routine manner. She was in her room the entire time except for a quick lunch around one o'clock. El Tigre did not see her or speak to her and she suspected that he was out taking care of his business. She knew very little at first about his business but a word here and a word there had increased her knowledge of it immeasurably. He seemed to have his hot little hands in every racket in Nueva Laredo—dope, women, bootleg whiskey, gambling—just about everything. At first this had bothered her, but as time passed she began to respect him for it. He was in his own way a big businessman, and at the same time he wasn't the potbellied type in the cartoons in left-wing newspapers. He was lean and strong, willing to take chances, willing to risk everything when he had to.

He was, in brief, the last outpost of rugged individualism left in the twentieth century. But whatever he was and wherever he was, the fact remained that she spent the morning and afternoon alone in her room.

She wasn't bored. There were things she had to do, and the most important thing was to prepare herself for him in the event that he might want her later that evening. Taking care of her face and body was a full-time job nowadays and one which she couldn't pass over lightly. As soon as she got back from breakfast she took a long and luxurious bath in her private bathroom with scent in her bathwater and with a special soap with a heavy oil base that did wonders for an already perfect complexion. She washed every area of her skin very thoroughly and very carefully, taking note of the bruises and black-and-blue marks on her body and hoping that they would be gone by nightfall.

As she soaped her breasts she was glad that the bruise on one of them had healed and that neither was black-and-blue at the moment. Her breasts were larger and firmer than ever and this surprised her, for at first she had thought that the beatings he gave her would break down the tissues and do permanent damage to her breasts. Apparently the reverse was true, and this was fortunate because he seemed to enjoy hurting her there more than anything else. She was very sensitive there, of course, and that one time when he had kicked her in the breast with his heavy leather boots on she thought she was going to die on the spot. But she was alive and her breasts were in excellent shape so there didn't seem to be anything to worry about—only the pain, and she had to admit that she liked the pain as much as he liked inflicting it.

Later that afternoon she put on her makeup. She used a little eyeshadow and a tiny bit of rouge to accent the color that was already present in her cheeks. She also used a very bright lipstick and put it on thickly because that was the way he liked it. He liked her to have enough lipstick on so that it got smeared all over the place when he kissed her. She also spent considerable time rubbing oils and creams into her skin so that it would be soft and creamy for him, soft and smooth and perfect.

Pandora, the seemingly ageless servant who was over forty and under a hundred but who could have been anywhere in-between, served her dinner in her room. Dinner that night was a thick sirloin, just the steak with more coffee to wash it down. After dinner she remained in her room while Pandora gathered up the dishes and vanished with them. She waited, hoping that he would call her, wondering what he would want her to do, itching for him and itching to know how the night would turn out, what they would do and what would happen.

It was one hell of a night.

Pandora knocked on the door at a quarter past nine. "You are to go to him," she said, which meant that El Tigre was waiting for her in the room where she had first been seduced. She was all dressed up in a sheer black cocktail gown with high-heeled pumps on her feet and she hurried down the hallway and down a flight of stairs to the bedroom.

El Tigre was in the bedroom. He was wearing a black silk robe, unembroidered except for his adopted coat-of-arms on the back of it. The coat-of-arms was a simple one—a shield with a rampant tiger holding a whip in one paw.

He was not alone,

There was a girl in the room, a little slip of a girl who couldn't have been more than fifteen if she was that old. She was very small and very young and very much afraid. She was also very naked.

She was lashed to a wrought iron frame that rested on the floor in the center of the room. The frame was an x-shaped affair and each of her arms was lashed to one of the top branches of the X and each of her legs to one of the legs of the frame. Her body was held at a forty-five degree angle to the floor.

She was crying softly.

El Tigre turned when Mona entered the room. "Come in," he told her. "And shut the door."

When she was inside and the door shut he said: "You are in time. Have you met our visitor?"

She shook her head. She was staring hard at the naked girl and she felt herself beginning to tremble.

El Tigre turned to the girl and bowed low, a mocking bow. "Miss Conchita Perez, may I present Mrs. Mona Sutton? Mrs. Sutton, Miss Perez."

The girl looked at Mona. The girl's eyes were wide with fear and her lips were parted as though she wished to say something but was unable to force out any words. Her skin was a soft golden color and she was a very lovely thing, Mona noticed. A very lovely thing—and a girl who most definitely did not belong here in a room with El Tigre. She belonged with her family, or at school, or almost anywhere other than where she was.

"Miss Perez is rather attractive, don't you agree?"

Mona turned to him. "Let her go," she said. "Please—let her go."

"Let her go? You mean that I should release her?"

"Yes."

"But why?"

"She doesn't belong here. Let her go."

He smiled. "But you are in error," he said. "She certainly does belong here. I have a bill of sale from her father which testifies quite precisely that she belongs here."

"A bill of . . ."

"A bill of sale," he repeated. "For the sum of one thousand pesos, or eight hundred American dollars, Señor Rafael Perez agreed to relinquish all paternal rights to one Conchita Perez, fourteen years of age."

"But—"

"But humans are not bought or sold? You have not been long in Mexico, Mona. The girl is my property, in fact if not in law. She will work for me."

"Doing what?"

"In one of the houses."

"You're going to make a prostitute out of her?"

He nodded as if it should have been obvious from the start that that was what he was going to do.

"You can't!"

"Of course I can."

"But she's so young—"

"Not too young. A young girl commands a higher price. By the time a prostitute is over twenty-five in this country she's no good any more. Girls mature at an early age; they become useless at an equally early age. In ten years this one will be earning a dollar a shot in one of the shacks at the side of the town. But now—"

"El Tigre—"

"Never interrupt me." The three words came from his lips like a bullet from a revolver. They cut her off and she couldn't even recall what she had been about to say.

"To return to the girl," he said. It was obvious that the girl had understood nothing of what they had been saying. She evidently spoke nothing but Spanish and the chattering in English was going completely over her head. But she knew that there was a good deal to fear.

"The girl," he repeated. "Conchita—" the girl's eyes opened wider at the mention of her name "—is, for better or for worse, a virgin. In some towns on the border it is the custom to offer a virgin to one of the *turistas* at a higher price. I have always felt that this is a barbarous practice. Such treatment can ruin a girl permanently."

For a moment she thought she was hearing things. What could he care if a girl was ruined permanently? What could he care if a human being was reduced to the level of an animal? But before she could say anything he explained himself.

"Ruined," he said. "A girl must be introduced to her work in the proper manner. A prostitute needs training just as any skilled worker does. You shall watch me train the girl tonight."

Her heart sank as she realized what he was talking about. She watched, spellbound and sick at the same time, as he walked toward the girl, watched the fear blaze a red flame in the girl's wide eyes, watched the horrible way in which the girl tried to draw away from him but couldn't because of the way she was tied.

El Tigre removed his robe. He was naked now and he was standing close enough to the girl so that he could reach out and touch her. Which was just what he did—his hand snaked out and his fingers closed around a soft young breast.

"Notice," he said. "Notice how firm and soft the flesh is at such an age. Notice how flawless the skin is upon the breasts." His tone was that of a lecturer, a professor explaining a finer point of a subject.

He turned to Mona. "Remove your clothing," he told her. "It unnerves me."

She didn't protest, didn't wait a moment to do as he told her.

She was well-trained by this time and she stripped at once to avoid the blow he would have given her otherwise.

"Come here."

She walked over to where he was standing. She watched as he touched the girl's breasts. "Touch her as I am touching her," he ordered.

Mona had never touched another girl's bosom before. She hesitated for the merest fraction of a second; it was too long. El Tigre's elbow dug into the side of her ribs and she doubled up in pain.

"Touch her!"

She reached out a hand, touched the girl's breast. He was right—the skin was very soft, the flesh firm.

"Nice?"

"Very nice," she agreed.

"Touch her in the other place."

No hesitation this time. Her hand responded automatically to the command. The girl tried to twist away from her hand but she couldn't move.

"Release her."

She did as she was told and took a step back.

"May I go now?"

"No. I want you to watch."

"I don't want to watch. I don't even want you to do it but I certainly don't want to watch."

"I didn't ask what you wanted."

She didn't say anything.

"Sit over there," he told her. "Sit where I can watch you. If you take your eyes off us for one second or if you make a single sound

I shall kill you. I shall kill you in a manner which I will not bother to describe, but it should suffice to say that it will take you a minimum of six days to die and that you shall be in pain every minute of the time."

She sat where he wanted her to sit. Her eyes were wide as he advanced upon the frightened girl and took hold of her. The girl's mouth was open for a scream but the scream stayed in her throat.

Then he touched her and hurt her and the scream came out. It was a thin, shrill scream and it went right through Mona. She wanted to scream too, to let out a wail they would hear in Hong Kong.

But she remained silent. She didn't forget what he had told her and she didn't doubt he would do what he had said he would do, and she remained silent and kept her eyes open while he took the girl forcefully and brutally, while the girl screamed her lungs out and bled like a stuck pig. She kept her eyes on the two of them while his eyes shone like stars and the girl wailed like a banshee, watched his pleasure and her pain until finally, finally after ages and ages it was over.

Afterwards he untied the girl and made love to her two more times in other ways. The girl didn't scream any more and by the time he was through with her she seemed almost accustomed to it all. Mona could see what was happening; in a week or two the girl would have accepted her fate. She would be a prostitute, a prostitute until she died, and never again would she attempt to repel a man. He had broken the girl in much the same manner that cowboys break mustangs to saddle. She had been given a liberal education in sexual calisthenics and she would have the rest of her life to practice what she had been taught.

When it was over he rang a bell. A servant—not Pandora but another equally ageless woman—appeared from nowhere and led the girl off. The woman's face was expressionless; she didn't seem to take any notice of what was happening or of what had already happened. Mona wondered how often this happened, how many times the woman had answered the summoning bell to lead a broken girl from the room.

El Tigre turned to her after the door was shut again and she thought: *Now it's my turn, now he wants me, wants something from me, and now it's my turn.*

"Come here."

She went to him. He looked weak now, as if the interlude with Conchita had exhausted him somehow. It was more than a physical exhaustion. It was as if something had been taken from within him.

He drew her close, pressed her body to his. His arms went around her and he buried his face in her hair, stroking the back of her hand. Without thinking she held him close, touched his shoulder, kissed the side of his neck.

They were both naked and their bodies together were warm and slippery with sweat. In spite of this there was nothing sexual about the embrace. On the contrary the whole little scene was strangely and uniquely sexless. He held her, his face buried in her hair, his hand holding her, his breath coming in long gasping pulls. She thought for a moment or two that he was about to faint but he didn't.

He released her finally, took her by the hand and led her to the circular bed. He sat down and indicated that she should sit beside him. They sat side by side, their bodies almost but not quite touching, their eyes looking across the room at the bare wall.

Finally he spoke.

"You and I," he said. "We should talk, I think. I think there are things we must say to each other."

She waited for him to go on.

"You think that I am a beast," he said. "It is true, of course. I become an animal. I need things too desperately, too insistently. I need to hurt people, to inflict pain. I have hurt you many times, have I not?"

She shrugged as if to indicate that it was nothing.

"No," he said. "I have hurt you very badly, yet you must know that I love you. Did you know that?"

"No."

"I do. You are the only woman I love. But I cannot love you the way a man normally loves a woman."

"I know."

"I am brutal," he went on. "I have had to be brutal. I have had to use my claws as well as my brains. I am El Tigre and I have had to use my claws on people. No longer can I live without using my claws. Do you understand me?"

"I think so."

"It is very abnormal," he said. "A few moments ago I told you that if you failed to watch me or if you let out a scream I would kill you. Do you remember? I was very much in love with you then, but if you had not obeyed me I would have gone through hell for six days and then you would have died, just as I said."

"I know."

"Love," he said, almost scornfully. "Love. This love of ours is a sickness. I love you and hurt you, and you would not love me if I were not the kind of man that I am. You take my beatings and you love me for them. If I failed to beat you you would fail to love me."

She nodded,

"We will destroy each other," he said. "It is a sickness that we have and in time one of us will kill the other. I will kill you or you will betray me or kill me and then it will be over. It is a disease."

She didn't say anything.

"What were you thinking earlier?"

"That you were a horrible brute."

"With the girl?"

She nodded.

"I was," he said. "But I can be worse. I have been worse. You have never seen me murder, have you?"

"No."

"You will. Someday you will be here and you will watch me kill a person, perhaps with a gun or with a razor or a knife, or perhaps with my hands, my claws. Have you ever seen anyone die?"

"Just from sickness."

"I mean a violent death. That is the only kind of death that I think of when I say death."

"No," she said. "I've never seen that."

"Would you like to?"

"No."

"Then you will. Not tonight, but sometime in the future. You will not like it but it shall happen."

She nodded.

"You will not like it. You will hate it but it will only make you love me more. You love me now, do you not?"

"Yes."

"You love me when I hurt you, do you not?"

"Yes."

He took the nipple of one of her breasts between the thumb and forefinger of his right hand and began to squeeze. He used his fingernails, his claws, and the pain was absolutely excruciating.

She didn't let out a sound.

"Do you still love me?"

"I love you."

"Even now?"

"More than ever."

He released her. He smiled, a very sad smile, and he lowered his mouth to the injured flesh and kissed it. It was a rare display of genuine tenderness and she was touched in spite of herself. She felt like crying. She put her hands on the back of his neck and stroked him there while he kissed her breast.

"You see? We are strange people."

"I know."

"What we have done, it is a beginning. I will be much more cruel to you in the future. I will hurt you terribly."

"I know."

"Do you think you can bear it?"

She nodded.

"Is it what you want?"

She nodded again.

"I am giving you a chance," he said slowly. "A final chance, a chance I will never give you after tonight. You may leave here tonight. You may pack your things and go away and we shall never see each other again. I had thought of you at first as a *Norteamericano* woman whom I would have once and that would be all. I did not expect love, not the type of love we have. If you wish to end it I am giving you the chance."

"I don't want it to end."

"It is your only chance," he said. "If you do not go now you will never be able to leave. I will kill you first."

"Where could I go?"

"To your husband."

"I don't have a husband."

"To your country then. To your home."

"This is my country. My home is wherever you are."

"You will stay then?"

"I will stay."

"Forever?"

"Forever."

He pushed her back down on the bed. "I want you now," he said. "I want you."

Then: "Do you like this?"

"Very much."

"And this?"

A wave of passion flowed over her, enveloped her, submerged her. This was a sort of lovemaking she had never experienced with him before, an infinitely tender sort of lovemaking, and she wanted to make it last because she knew that it would be long before he was like this again. In the future he would be brutal once more, injuring her, hurting her, but now he was tender and loving and she wanted to draw out the moment as long as possible.

His hands, his lips, his arms, his legs, his strong hard young body. God, how she loved him!

They kissed and her tongue explored the inside of his mouth, then withdrew. She lay completely passive now while his hands worked on her, coaxing her to a breathtaking peak of passion. She closed her eyes tight and let her whole body go entirely limp.

"This. Do you like this?"

"I love it," she said.

And: "I love you. Oh, God!"

Chapter 8

Sutton woke up with a bed beneath him, a ceiling above him and four walls around him. The bed was a lumpy mattress that rested on a dirty bare wood floor that hadn't been scrubbed in years. The ceiling was missing plaster and the walls were pock-marked where the paint had peeled from them. Sutton woke up, took no notice of the condition of mattress or ceiling or walls or floor, rolled over and reached for a bottle.

The bottle was cheap wine. The wine cost a dollar a gallon stateside and somewhat less in Mexico and this may give some small indication of its approximate quality. If its alcohol content were somewhat higher it would have been marked *Unfit For Human Consumption* and would have been used exclusively to sterilize surgical instruments.

But Sutton didn't think about the quality of the wine any more than he thought about the condition of his room. The wine was his food and the room was his home and nothing more had to be taken into consideration. There was a half-inch worth of wine in the bottom of the gallon jug and he downed it in one long and painful swallow. Then, and only then, did he entirely come to life.

It was morning or afternoon or evening or night. He didn't know which and he didn't care, nor would he find out until he left the room and went outside. The room had no windows and this suited Sutton one hundred percent. It fitted in with the type of life he was leading, a life in which days were not divided into mornings and afternoons and evenings and nights. Sutton slept when there was enough alcohol in his bloodstream to get him to sleep; he woke up when the alcohol wore off and his body came back to life. It did not matter whether the sun was shining or not, whether driving rain or unbearable heat was the condition outside. His mode of living did not take these factors into consideration. All that mattered was the level of wine in the jug and the percentage of alcohol in his bloodstream.

He struggled to sit up, then pitched the now empty jug across the room. It caromed off the wall and skidded around on the floor before it came to rest but Sutton knew that no one else in the building would give a damn how much noise it made. The building was the home of other bums like Sutton—broken-down pimps and gamblers, rum-dumb winos, people who had either given up or might just as well. People who were waiting to die.

Sutton hauled himself up from the mattress. He was naked and he fumbled around for clothing. All his clothes were dirty but it had been so long since he had worn clean clothing that he didn't even stop to think about it. He dressed as quickly as he could, picking clothes at random from the floor and putting them on. His socks didn't match and his shoes were worn and streaked with his own vomit. The cuffs of his trousers were frayed and so was the collar on his shirt. This didn't bother him. It was quite apparent that very few things bothered Sutton.

Not even the face in the mirror in the washroom down the hall bothered him, and this was surprising when he realized that it was his own face and that he did not recognize it at first. The mouth was missing three front teeth and half of another one, the forehead was decorated with an inch-and-a-half long gash clotted with dried blood, the cheeks and chin and neck were ragged with stubble nearly an inch long. If the rest of him had been in better shape one might have guessed that he was growing a beard. However, despite the length of his beard, it was obvious that he was not growing a beard. He was simply not shaving, and there is a difference.

"*Pobrecito,*" he said to the mirror image. *Poor little one*, he thought, but he thought it in Spanish. He spoke Spanish now, not fluently to be sure but enough to make himself understood and to understand others if they spoke slowly. He had made no effort to learn the language. It had come to him, along with the filth and the alcoholism and everything else. He had absorbed it through the pores of his skin.

He left the building, nodding to a person or two on the way out, and discovered when he hit the street that it was around noon with the sun high in the sky. He fumbled in his pocket for a few coins, found enough for a glass of wine and went to the bar on the corner. The wine was the same abysmal stuff that had been in the jug at his bedside but he sipped the glassful without a single shudder, located more coins and bought another.

He had called the mirror image *Pobrecito* but over the second glass of wine he had to admit that he was not so damned unfortunate. In several respects he was one of the lucky ones and he thought about those several aspects for a moment or two and felt good about them.

There was, for one thing, the indescribable security of having hit absolute bottom. It is a sort of security which both merits and defies description. No matter what might happen to him he could not sink any further. No matter what he did he could not possibly louse things up. Things were already loused up, totally and irretrievably loused up, loused up for now and forever.

The beauty of absolute failure is that any additional failure is quite impossible.

Secondly there was the lack of problems. He had but one problem—the problem of securing enough wine daily to keep body and soul together. And even this was a small problem because almost any American tourist would come through with two bits or half a buck for a fellow American. His living costs were low—four dollars a week for his room, a dollar a day or so for wine, and an occasional dollar for a woman.

At first there had been no problem at all in this respect because he had the money from the car that he sold in Laredo. But the money weighted him down and he was glad when it was gone. He had to worry about having it stolen and he was sick and tired of worrying, so he spent it as fast as he could, going every night to the sex shows, buying drinks for everybody around him, tipping waiters and bartenders and whores and pimps, getting rid of the money as fast as possible. When it was gone he was able to breathe easier. The money from the car was the last line with the past, the last line with the ad game and the house in Connecticut and, of course, with Mona.

He rarely thought of her now and when he did it was without hatred or love, sorrow or bitterness or any emotion whatsoever. The notion that an alcoholic's life enabled him to forget was, he discovered, not quite true. He remembered everything but the memories were so blurred, so jumbled, that they rarely if ever disturbed him. The most distorted part of it all was his sense of time. He remembered persons, events, places, but he could hardly ever place them in the proper chronological order. They were all just random memories in the ashbin that was his mind, empty persons and places and things that his brain picked up and looked at and discarded.

He remembered that redhead—what was her name? That's right, Marie Something, Marie Wilts or Wilks or Wilkie; it didn't matter. He remembered that they had returned to the sex show, that they had watched and imitated and improvised, that they had left to drink some more and found a room to make love some more and finally slept.

Then what had happened? She had vanished, vanished, somewhere, gone from him, to somebody else or simply disappeared into the earth. She was gone, to hell with her, she didn't matter, nobody did, and so on.

Other memories. More sex, more liquor. A two-day high on peyote with Ernesto, the guide. The high had been accomplished in a convenient manner—he had paid for the peyote and in return Ernesto had instructed him in its use. The stuff was the bud from a certain species of cactus and Ernesto cut up the buds into tiny pieces and they divided them up and chewed and swallowed them. The peyote had a foul taste, horribly bitter, and it took him awhile before he got some down without gagging.

When they were high time stood still. Movement, activity of any sort, all became completely unnecessary. He sat for hours at a time staring into space and thinking deep and shapeless thoughts, lost in himself and in the universe, lost and unafraid and uncaring.

It lasted for two days—then he came down from the effects of the peyote and he was starving; he hadn't had anything to eat in 48 hours and his stomach was howling in his ears.

How long had it been? How long since the final scene with Mona, the final break, the sale of the car and the move from the Plaza to the unnamed rattrap on the Mexican side of the Rio Grande? He honestly didn't know—time was meaningless and he was not even sure what month it was now and couldn't remember in what month it had all started. He was a bum, a wino, a *borracho*.

When the second glass of wine was finished he started to order a third but had no money to pay for it. His legs were steadier now and he was able to walk easily out of the bar and onto the street outside. He headed toward the small park on the west side of the town. Alcoholics were forbidden in the main plaza but few tourists frequented the park on the west side and a wino could sit there without being disturbed.

On the way to the park he hustled a tourist for a nickel for cigarettes. Mexican cigarettes, the cheaper brand, were only fifty centavos a pack and he had a penny left over. A penny was a penny and he tucked it carefully into the pocket of his shirt. He reached the park and found an empty bench, sat down and smoked one of the cigarettes. The wine had warmed him inside and the hot sun outside made him sleepy. He finished the cigarette, smoking it all the way down until he would have burned his fingers if he smoked any more. Then he threw the tiny butt into the gutter and leaned back and closed his eyes.

He didn't exactly sleep. When you sit upright on a park bench you do not exactly sleep, any more than you sleep in a bus or a subway. He dozed, woke and dozed again. His mind roamed around in concentric circles and his eyes would open periodically, gaze at the world for a second or two, and then close once again. It was very restful, very relaxing. He sat in the sun and felt very lazy and very much at peace with the world. No one bothered him, no shoeshine boys pestered him to hire them, nobody attempted to sell him anything. A tourist in a public park had to fight off a mass of peddlers offering everything from cheap costume jewelry to feelthy pictures and Spanish fly, but Sutton was no longer a tourist and the Mexicans knew it. They let him doze.

At seven the sun was not so hot and an occasional breeze chilled him. Besides, it was high time he got some more alcohol into his bloodstream. He woke up thoroughly, stretched his muscles to get them in shape for the walk back to the center of town, and pulled himself up from the bench.

He smoked two more cigarettes on the way back, walking easily. After he had finished the second cigarette the walk was beginning to get him down and the need for more wine was becoming a physical as well as a mental need. He stopped several tourists on the way but pickings were not as good as usual. Nobody gave him anything and one middle-aged woman with a Midwestern accent told him he was a disgrace to his nation. She made it sound as though she was going to introduce a resolution at the next local DAR meeting to have him certified un-American, or something. He gave her a biologically impossible suggestion, got a mild kick out of the way her face went white at the words, and ambled off toward the plaza.

When he saw the two young men he knew that he was going to get some wine.

There were two of them but they looked so much alike that he figured they did it with mirrors. They were both about six feet tall, dressed in short-sleeve white sport shirts and khaki pants. They had blond hair cropped very short and they were wearing desert boots on their feet. They were, quite obviously, a pair of college students out on the town, and Sutton was willing to give odds they were from one of the Ivy League colleges. They had that look about them. They looked as though they had just been peeled.

He approached them slowly, thinking as he walked that a pair like these two might be good for one hell of a lot of wine if he played his cards right. They looked over at him with a certain amount of curiosity and he gave them a smile and said, "Hello, fellows. How would you like to buy an old bum a drink?"

One of them laughed. "You mean you don't want a dime for a cup of coffee?"

"Hell, no. What would I do with coffee?"

This time they both laughed. "Jeff," one of them said, "what say we buy the old guy a drink?"

"*A* drink?" Jeff shook his head soberly. "Richard my boy, I think we have a fellow Princeton man here. No Princeton man's going to be content with *a* drink. Let's buy him a goddamned *batch* of drinks."

"Splendid," said Richard.

"Where to, old man? Where's a good place to drink?"

Sutton led them to one of the better bars and they took a table near the window. The two Princeton boys were very pleased to have come across Sutton—they seemed slightly bored with the town and he promised to be mildly amusing. The one called Jeff ordered a round of Scotches and Sutton drank his quickly. It had been so long since he had had good liquor that he hardly remembered what it tasted like.

"To Old Nassau," he toasted, hoping vaguely that they still called Princeton "Old Nassau."

"To Old Nassau," they echoed in mock gravity. Three glasses clinked and three shots of Scotch disappeared down three throats.

"Knew you for a Princeton man," Jeff explained over the second round of drinks. "Took one look at you and I said to myself, *There's a Princeton man.*"

"You can always tell a Princeton man," Richard added. He didn't explain just *how* you could always tell a Princeton man but waved at the waiter for another round. It was better than an explanation.

"Richard just turned twenty-one," Jeff said over the third round of drinks. "His grandfather left him a legacy of ... well, a very large legacy. Left it years ago but old Richard had to wait until he was twenty-one to get it."

"And you're celebrating?"

"Celebrating," said Richard, "is hardly the word for it. We're doing the whole bloody country of Mexico."

"How long have you been in Laredo?"

"Just got in yesterday. Staying over at the Plaza."

Sutton nodded absently. He and Mona had stayed at the Plaza. How long ago had that been? He couldn't remember and he didn't say anything.

"From here we go to Mexico City. Got reservations at the best hotel there, whatever the hell the name of it is. You remember, Jeff?"

Jeff shook his head.

"Then Acapulco. A month lying on the beach and going to the nightclubs and sleeping with the finest young flowers of Mexico. Should be a ball, wouldn't you say?"

Sutton nodded sagely.

"Only thing," Jeff said over the fourth round of drinks. "Only thing is that this town is as dead as a doornail. Not that I've seen too many doornails. Ever seen a doornail, Sutton?"

"Never," said Sutton.

"What we need," Richard said, "is entertainment. Life. Happiness. Excitement. *Joie de vivre. Viva Castro.* You know."

Sutton nodded.

"We were thinking," Jeff said, "that you might know the town."

"This town?"

"This town."

"Hell," said Sutton, "I guess I've been around it long enough. You want me to show you around?"

"Well, we're not exactly looking for a guided tour. I thought there might be something special—"

"You mean women?"

"Ah," said Jeff expansively. "Ah, I *knew* you were a Princeton man. Nobody but a Princeton man could have such perception. Nobody but a Princeton man could see through to the very depths of another man's soul, could so accurately plumb the forty fathoms of a man's complex motivations."

"You mean women," said Sutton.

"We mean women," said Jeff.

"Not just women," Richard explained. "We are young, but we *are* Princeton men."

"And have had women," Jeff said.

"Not a countless number of women," Richard said. "A townie or two in New Jersey, a coed or two at Vassar, a harlot or two in New York—"

"A housewife or two in Levittown, a chambermaid or two at the St. Regis, a poetess or two in the Village—"

"A high school girl or two in Poughkeepsie, a waitress or two at Lake Placid, a beat chick or two in Frisco—"

"A female sheep or two in Montana—"

Richard shuddered.

"What we're getting at," said Jeff, "is that we thought you might have something special on tap. One hears a lot of stories about border towns, you know. Stories about exotic pleasures and all that."

"What we're getting at," said Richard, "is that, as one Princeton man to another—"

"One Princeton man to *two* others, to be precise—"

"That you might be able to show us the wilder side of Nueva Laredo. The part the ordinary tourists miss out on."

Sutton had an idea.

"Something unique," Jeff said. "Money doesn't much matter as we have quite a good deal of it. If you could lead us to a really original sort of experience—"

Sutton let a smile cross his face. He was feeling the drinks now and he was at peace with the world, at peace with himself, at peace with his two benefactors.

"Gentlemen," he said. "Fellow Princeton men—have you ever been to a sex show?"

The boys brightened. "Sutton," Richard said, "you are a jewel."

"A diamond."

"In a platinum setting."

"It's expensive," Sutton pointed out.

"Is it worth it?"

He nodded.

"Then hang the expense! Is it far from here?"

"Not very far."

"Good! Does it start soon?"

"In a few minutes."

"Excellent! Can you watch it with a girl?"

"It costs an extra twenty-five dollars."

"Hang the twenty-five dollars! Will you come with us?"

Sutton thought about the shows he had seen and his pulse quickened at the thought of seeing another one. While alcohol had dimmed the need for a woman the idea of watching a sex show had him more than mildly interested.

"I can't afford it," he said, hinting.

"*Afford it*? You can't afford Scotch, either. As one Princeton man to another, Sutton, will you be our guest?"

"I would be delighted."

The boys sprang up from the table. "Sutton," Jeff cried, "lead on!"

And away they went.

Sutton zeroed in on the place with the instinct of a homing pigeon. With Jeff on one side and Richard on the other he pressed the buzzer and waited until the door was opened by the inevitable neat young man in the inevitable brown suit. A smile of recognition that was so quick as to be almost imperceptible flashed across the face of the neat young man.

"These are my friends," Sutton explained, truthfully enough. "College chums," he added. And then he arranged the business details, but now he spoke Spanish. It was almost as convenient for him as English and he wanted to make the whole process vaguely mysterious.

"You will observe," he heard Jeff whispering, "the manner in which the true Princeton man is able to absorb the language and culture of a foreign nation in short order. I think our friend merits a monogram in the *Princetonian*."

Sutton smiled gently.

The business details were quickly arranged. Each of the boys was to have a private compartment and private female. Sutton was also to be supplied with his own compartment and woman. The sum of five hundred American dollars would cover the total cost of the evening's entertainment. One of the boys paid the full sum instantly without a murmur and a barefoot young lady arrived to escort each to his proper compartment. There was an awkward moment when Richard assumed that the young lady was to be his companion and acted upon the assumption by slipping one hand into her kimono and manipulating her rather appealing breasts, but things were set straight easily enough.

Within a few moments Sutton was alone in his own compartment. He glanced around for a minute or two, looked through the glass out onto the stage, drew a deep breath or two and began to remove his clothing. He was an old hand at the look-see game, as the sex shows were known in the Laredo skid row, and this time he didn't wait for the girl to enter before undressing. As he took off his clothes he felt a vague wish of pity for the poor prostitute who would have to entertain an old wino like himself this evening. The hell with it, he thought. Maybe she would be getting the better end anyway—she wouldn't have nearly as much work with an old sot than one of the Princeton boys would have been able to give her.

The girl who came in seconds later was taller than the general run of Mexican prostitutes. She took off her kimono and Sutton had to catch his breath—she was an exceptionally lovely thing with firm high breasts and full sensuous hips. And she seemed to like her work. Without a hint of shyness or modesty she came over to Sutton and rubbed her soft belly against him, working her big breasts against his chest. He ran his hand over and down her back, cupped her firm buttocks with both hands and pressed her close.

The lights in the compartments dimmed. The stage lights came on to illuminate the empty stage. Sutton lowered himself into the chair and drew the girl down with him so that she was sitting up in his lap with one luscious breast pressed against his right cheek.

The trapdoor opened,

Two women came on stage.

One of the women was small, young, dark, lovely. But Sutton, whose eyes were suddenly wide with shock, hardly noticed her. His eyes were on the other woman, the second one to appear through the trapdoor.

She was tall, light in complexion, blonde. And her blonde hair was quite obviously her own. There was something familiar about her, something that became more and more familiar until Sutton's chest was encased in steel and he couldn't breathe.

He couldn't believe what he saw.

CHAPTER 9

The girl was very young and very soft and very naked. She stood in the middle of the stage knowing that many men were watching her but she was not nervous at all. Weeks ago she would have been nervous, terrified, but what she had gone through since then had turned her into a girl old beyond her years, a girl who was as tough inside as she was soft outside, a girl who was prepared for just about anything. While she appeared to be reticent and even a bit scared it was no more than the role she was playing, and inside where it counted she was firm, ready and almost excited.

Her name was Conchita Perez.

The woman, the blonde woman, was older and more experienced. She stood on the stage and looked like an Egyptian goddess about to exact a horrible sacrifice from a believer. She seemed sure of herself, confident, happily expectant. She was none of these things.

She was overwhelmingly conscious of each of the observers although she could see none of them. She felt the heat from each pair of eyes that was fastened upon her, felt the desire raging in dozens of loins, and her palms were damp with the cold sweat of fear. She was, in sum, the complete reverse of the girl on the stage with her.

Her name was Mona Sutton.

Just half an hour ago she had learned the part she was to play that evening. El Tigre told her himself, told her most explicitly what she was to do and how she was to do it and with whom she would share the spotlight. At first she hadn't believed him. Then, when she began to realize that he was speaking the truth, she attempted to laugh it off. She was nervous while she laughed but she forced the laughter from her lips and threw back her head.

The laughter accounted for the ugly bruise on her right breast just an inch or so to the left of the nipple.

Then she argued. He had dozens of performers he could summon, dozens of professional prostitutes who would be glad to perform on stage. She wouldn't even be any good. She would be horrible—she had never had anything to do with another woman and the mere thought of doing the sickening things that he wanted her to do made her nauseous.

The argument accounted for the raw red stripe across both her buttocks.

Then she begged. She would do anything, anything but that. She would go on the stage, she pleaded, but not with a woman. Anything but that. She wasn't a lesbian, couldn't begin to pretend she was a lesbian, couldn't stomach the notion of behaving like a lesbian.

With a sneer he told her that it wasn't as if she would be making love to a woman she had never met before. The girl in question was Conchita, he explained, and she knew Conchita. She had watched him rape Conchita and she certainly ought to feel close to the girl. He could understand, he said gently. He could understand her resentment at the notion of performing with a stranger.

But did she not agree that this was different?

She had lost and she knew that she had lost. Once more he went over the actions that he expected from her and this time she listened carefully so that she would not forget what she was supposed to do. Her mind protested that the actions were unnatural, sickening, but she no longer felt sick to her stomach. She was numb now, dead inside, and she merely nodded her head from time to time and committed his instructions to memory.

And now she was standing there and Conchita was a few feet from her, her back arched slightly, her young breasts alive and proud, her eyes saying that she was beginning to get impatient for the fun to begin. Fun? Oh, it would be loads of fun. Bushels of fun. Barrels of fun. Tons of fun. It would be a real thrill—like dying, say. Like going over Niagara Falls in a wheelbarrow.

Sure.

Her legs were unsteady as she moved forward and took the more-than-willing girl in her arms. She kissed the girl, probed Conchita's mouth with her tongue, stroked Conchita's buttocks with her hands.

Conchita pressed up against her and Mona felt the brand new sensation of another girl's breasts pressing against her own breasts, tasted another girl's mouth with her own mouth, felt another girl's belly against her own belly. She was sweating freely now and her skin was damp where it pressed against the softness of the girl.

She released Conchita, then straightened up and drew the girl's mouth to her own breasts. This wasn't so bad—as Conchita's soft lips worked on her she could close her eyes and almost imagine that it was a man who was doing these things to her instead of a girl.

Her nipples hardened and in spite of herself she felt the passion welling up within her. Conchita's hand was touching her now, touching her and stroking her, and she found it hard to fight the actual sexual desire that was building up within her.

Then Conchita let go of her.

Now it was her turn.

The desire left her as spontaneously as it had come. Now it was Mona who had to touch and kiss the breasts of Conchita. Her head reeled as she did it and she felt a wave of nausea come over her. She forced herself to go on, forced herself to ignore the natural revulsion for the unnatural caress. She kissed, she touched, and Conchita began to moan softly like a female dog in heat.

Then the next part.

The part that horrified her.

She let go of Conchita and the girl straightened up and placed her hands on her hips. Her eyes were on fire and her hips were thrust forward as if making an obscene offering to an insatiable goddess. Her feet were about a yard apart on the wooden floor and her head was thrown back with unmistakable abandon.

Mona shuddered, knowing as she did so that the audience probably mistook the shudder of nausea for a spasm of pure pleasure. She ran her hand over the girl's body, starting at the throat and moving downward very slowly.

Conchita trembled with delight.

Mona took a deep breath, released it. Her heart was pounding and her legs were more than unsteady. She half-hoped that she would faint dead away, half-wished for real death, the soft kiss of death that would relieve her permanently of a duty she would have done anything to avoid.

She didn't faint.

Nor did she die.

Instead, sick and disgusted with herself and with Conchita and with the world, sick and delirious, she lowered herself to the stage and kneeled in readiness at the feet of the Mexican girl.

Jeffrey Addison Beale was sublimely happy.

It did not take too much to make Jeffrey Addison Beale sublimely happy. All it took, as a matter of fact, was enough sensual pleasure in one form or another to make Jeffrey Addison Beale forget what an intolerable bore Jeffrey Addison Beale's life was.

The best prep school. The best home, the best family, the best social connections, the best debutantes to dance with at the best deb parties and occasionally to fondle in the best back seats, the best eating club at Princeton . . .

The list was endless. The best sports car to drive around in, the best charge accounts and credit cards, the best hotels and the best clothing and . . .

Oh, to hell with it. It was, fundamentally, a deadly bore, a lifetime of living a part and playing a role and being a prig, which last word Jeffrey Addison Beale frequently mispronounced and spelled with an extra letter when referring to himself.

But now—now life was good. The fluffy piece of tail which he was holding on his lap was definitely good and the incredible things she was doing were even better. Her name, she had announced solemnly, was Lola, and whatever Lola wanted she was going to get. He wasn't sure just what she might happen to want but he knew damned well what she was going to get.

And the spectacle! Those two women on the stage were marvelous, just marvelous. The sight of them made a man want to spend the rest of his life in Mexico. It damn near made him want to spend the rest of his life right in that little cubicle with his eyes glued to the window.

Magnificent!

Jeffrey Addison Beale watched the two women, watched them do amazing things, and all the while stroked the pert little behind of Miss Lola.

Finally he had seen enough.

Abruptly he stood up. The girl who had been in his lap was now on the floor with a very startled expression on a very pretty face. He smiled at her, then arranged her arms and legs in what he deemed a suitable position.

"Hang onto your hat," he said, knowing full well that she didn't understand a word of English and also knowing full well that she wasn't wearing a hat, or anything else.

"Hang onto your hat," he repeated, liking the sound of it. "This one's going to be a dilly!"

It was.

While Sutton sat in the chair with the girl in his arms and his eyes staring out through the glass, a very strange and entirely unique thing happened.

In the first place, he died.

In the second place, he was reborn.

A rebirth in any event is a rather miraculous event. It usually consists of a shot of emotional adrenalin applied to the heart and soul of a person. At one moment he is a wreck in one way or another; then something reinvigorates him and he is born anew.

This doesn't happen often but it does happen. It is rare, and miraculous, but it happens.

What happened to Sutton is somehow different.

You see, to begin with, he died. The entity that was Sutton suddenly ceased to exist. Its emotional heart stopped beating and its emotional blood stopped circulating. It just wasn't.

And for the briefest flash of time there was nothing at all.

Then there was a new man. The new man was Sutton, of course. But the new man had a new heart and new lungs and a new liver. The new man was alive with the blood racing in his veins and his heart pounding like a pneumatic hammer, with iron bands for legs and sledgehammer fists, with a keen brain and an utterly unshakeable will.

The new Sutton remembered the old Sutton. But it didn't seem possible that they had been the same person. And of course they hadn't—the one replaced the other. The new Sutton realized that there had been a weakling before, a spineless jellyfish who lived on wine and slept in dung, a filthy weakling who wasn't worth the space he occupied.

But the new Sutton did not hate the old Sutton. He held a good deal of contempt for him but the contempt could not be confused with hate. The old Sutton had been a self-hater but he was dead now.

Besides, the hatred of the new Sutton was entirely directed toward one individual. The individual who was responsible, directly or indirectly, for his death and rebirth, the individual who was responsible for the nauseating spectacle taking place upon the stage, the individual who had turned Sutton's wife into a whore and Sutton into a snail without a shell.

He had never met the man he hated. He had heard the name from Mona that last day they had been together; since then he had heard the name again a countless number of times. The man had a reputation in Laredo. His power was almost absolute, his holdings vast. Sutton knew that the man owned most of the bars in the town, controlled all the houses of prostitution and the bulk of the gambling, and was gradually gaining control of nearly every legitimate enterprise around. He had the money and the muscle to take over any property that interested him, whether it was a restaurant or a whorehouse or a woman.

The man, of course, was El Tigre.

And Sutton knew now that he was going to kill him. He didn't know how or when or where but those were details and details were unimportant. He wouldn't have known El Tigre if he stepped on him but that was just a minor obstacle—it wouldn't stand in his way. Sutton was a new man, a reborn man, a man with a mission.

Nothing would stand in his way.

His alcoholism was a physiological fact but he knew with total assurance that he would not have another drink until El Tigre was dead by his hand. He did not have a centavo to his name but he knew that he would somehow live to bring off the deed, would somehow get hold of everything he needed for the act. A bum had died and a superman had been born, and it is very difficult to chain a superman.

Sutton was a superman.

He watched the two women on the stage until they had finished what they were doing and had left the stage through the trapdoor. At one point the girl with him, who he had up to this point forgotten, began to attempt to excite him. He brushed her away and made her leave. "Go away," he told her in Spanish. "I'm going to need all the energy at my disposal. I can't waste any on you."

She seemed to understand. At any rate she left him alone, and when the two women had concluded their routine he got up and left the room. He got out of the building without saying a word to anybody, striding down the street with the directness and purposefulness which is to be found in madmen and supermen and in nobody else.

And Sutton was both.

Chapter 10

The sun had arisen before Richard Bellwether Stark III had finished what he was doing. Richard Bellwether Stark III had never had quite so much fun in his life, if the truth be known, and he was consequently as happy as a nymphomaniac on a flagpole. He had just finished making love to a very lovely little whore for the seventh time, which was a record even for Richard Bellwether Stark III. To complete the evening, four of the seven times were conducted in methods entirely new to Richard Bellwether Stark III. One of them was even new to the whore—he had made it up on the spot and it had worked magnificently.

He met Jeff in the hallway. They left the building at once and began talking earnestly, praising the evening and the floorshow and the women and their own impressive potencies. They reached the center of town before it occurred to Richard that they were missing Sutton.

"Hey," he said brilliantly, "we're missing Sutton!"

"Oh," said Jeff.

"Could he have walked out on us?"

"Not good old Sutton."

"Hardly. Poor son of a bitch could hardly walk to begin with."

"Maybe the evening was too much for him," Jeff suggested.

"Not in the best physical shape, you know. The excitement might have killed the poor bastard."

"Not Sutton. Not a Princeton man."

"You figure he really was a Princeton man?"

"Had to be. Good man, Sutton."

"Great man."

"Great Princeton man. Capital fellow."

"Say, I bet I know what happened to him."

"What?"

"Use your head, old man. He's a Princeton man, right?"

"Right."

"So he's probably still there going at it."

"Obviously," Richard said. "Obviously."

"Didn't you enjoy it?"

She just looked at him. She was still sick inside and all the vomiting hadn't managed to empty her of the sick feeling inside her. It didn't do any good, because every time she closed her eyes she remembered every detail of every embrace, every sensation and every thought and every caress. Now she was lying on the bed in her room, still naked and still sick, and he was standing by the side of the bed wearing his black robe and looking down upon her with a terrible smile on his face.

"No," she said unnecessarily. "I didn't like it."

"It was a new experience, was it not?"

She didn't say anything.

"As for me," he went on, "I rather enjoyed it. I've never seen you make love to anyone before, much less a girl. It was entertaining.

In addition, I have always felt that there is nothing quite so aesthetically pleasing as the sight of two women making love. There's a purity that I associate with women—"

"What would you know about purity?"

"At least as much as you do, if only because of my own remoteness from it. As I was attempting to say, Mona, there is a purity about two women making love. It delights the senses and the mind as well. It makes a man feel good inside. Do you understand me?"

She didn't answer him.

"Especially," he added, "when one of them hates it. When the one who is playing the role of the aggressor hates it, then it is especially delighting to me. And you hated it, didn't you?"

"I loathed it."

She closed her eyes again and let herself remember it. She loathed it, had loathed it completely, and as much as she had loathed it had Conchita enjoyed it. Mona was sure that the girl had reached climax at least twice from caresses that brought nothing but nausea to Mona and all this somehow made the thing worse. She tried to match the girl she had made love to with the poor frightened virgin she had watched El Tigre rape and the two pictures seemed incompatible. Perhaps the treatment Conchita had received from men had turned her into a lesbian; perhaps the girl had just become a human sex machine who enjoyed all sexual contact to the nth degree. It didn't matter, she decided.

When she opened her eyes El Tigre had removed his robe. He stood towering over her for a moment, then picked up his robe and put it on again.

"After your little exhibition," he said, "I wanted you very

much. But you have been through too much, my dear. Too much in one night is not good. I will leave you."

He started for the door and she knew what she was going to do, knew it in advance and fought it but couldn't help herself. Suddenly she wanted him, wanted him more than she had ever wanted him before and wanted him while she hated the thought of him.

"Stay," she said.

"Why?"

"Make love to me."

"You want me to?"

"Yes."

His eyes said that he had known all along that she would call him back. He returned to the bedside, tossed his robe on the floor and climbed into bed with her.

His lovemaking was forceful and direct and to the point. There were no preliminaries, no caresses, no words or slaps or blows—nothing, in short, but his body and her body behaving in a way that was as old as mankind. She held him tight and loved him with every bit of her being, loved him and hated him at once, loved him and hated him and moved with him, loved him and hated him and held him inside of her, loved him and hated him and loved him and hated him and . . .

She cried out at the climax. She shrieked—one thin high shriek that lasted for only a second. Then her whole body went limp and her arms hung at her sides like two slabs of beef. He was heavy on top of her and she pushed him away because he was too heavy.

Her eyes were closed now and she was lying on top of the bed like a corpse. The lovemaking was, of course, the ultimate humiliation, the last word in nausea. First he made her beg for him, then he made love to her superbly, and now he had turned away from her and was putting on his robe again. God, how she hated him!

And it was then that he said very seriously, "You hate me, don't you?"

"Yes."

"Very much?"

"Completely."

"But you also love me, don't you?"

She turned away.

"Don't you?"

She turned back to him and her voice was a whisper when she spoke. "Of course I do," she said. "I always will."

CHAPTER 11

Sometimes it is not enough to be a man with a mission. When nothing exists but the man and the job, when the essential tools are sadly lacking, all the determination in the world may not be enough. Washington would have had a devil of a time crossing the Delaware without a boat, Caesar could hardly have swum the Rubicon, and all the blood and sweat and tears in creation wouldn't have saved a Britain deprived of American lend-lease. The man and the mission are seemingly not enough; the wherewithal is also necessary.

But people manage. The nameless stalwart who carried a message to Garcia was one who managed.

Sutton was determined to be another.

He didn't have a cent or a centavo. His clothing was falling apart and his physical condition was just a step or two away from eternity. Without alcohol—and he had sworn off alcohol that night in the compartment—it was doubtful that he could remain alive, let alone kill El Tigre.

Killing El Tigre was hard enough to begin with. Sutton didn't know the man by sight and had no idea where he lived. He didn't have a gun or a knife or any implement of destruction nor did he have the money to buy anything. Killing El Tigre was in short well nigh impossible.

But Sutton was going to kill him.

It was night and he was alone in the empty streets of Nueva Laredo. The streets were not entirely empty—life in a border town goes on twenty-four hours a day, seven days a week, and the pimps were still pimping and the whores still whoring and the peddlers still peddling even if the sky was dark and it was after four in the morning. Sutton walked up one street and down another, up another and down still another, going nowhere but walking very purposefully, very determinedly, not knowing just where he was going but anxious to get there as quickly as possible.

Item one—he had to find El Tigre.

Item two—he had to get hold of something to kill him with.

Item three—he had to kill him.

When he sat down on a bench in the plaza he sat down not because he was tired of walking but because he thought that he would be able to concentrate better sitting down. He was not tired in the least and he could have walked for endless miles without tiring. His whole nervous and muscular system was so completely fixed upon one objective that exhaustion could not come to him until the objective was achieved. He might die, might collapse and die of malnutrition or lack of sleep, but death would come to him before tiredness.

Item one—he had to find El Tigre.

This would not be so easy. But, he decided, it would not be so hard either. One simply had to ask people where he was and force them to tell him.

The person he asked would not wish to divulge the information. El Tigre was shrouded in secrecy and discussed in whispers and no man would want to reveal information about him.

The man whom Sutton selected as his informer would have to be bribed or forced. Sutton had nothing to bribe anybody with. Therefore force was necessary. And, as he thought about it, the process became simple enough. He would find his pigeon and threaten to kill the pigeon if the pigeon did not talk. If the pigeon talked all was well. If not, he would kill him and look for another pigeon.

Now all he had to do was find a talking pigeon.

Precisely four minutes and thirty-seven seconds after he had figured out this mode of operation Ernesto strolled through the park. *Ernesto the pigeon*, Sutton thought instantly, and he whispered: "Ernesto!"

The Mexican turned.

"*Venga aqui*," Sutton said. "Come here."

Ernesto came over.

"Sit down."

Ernesto sat down.

"Where may I find El Tigre?"

Ernesto's face was impassive. He acted as though he had not even heard the question but Sutton knew that he had heard and understood perfectly. He repeated the question, louder this time, and a troubled look came to the guide's face.

"You should not speak of El Tigre," Ernesto said. "It is forbidden. It is also dangerous."

"Where is El Tigre?"

"I cannot say."

"You do not know?"

An instant's hesitation indicated that Ernesto definitely did know.

"Tell me."

"I cannot."

Calmly, his whole body completely relaxed, Sutton reached for the Mexican's arm and wrapped his own arm around it so that the slightest increase in pressure would be enough to break the arm.

"Tell me."

Ernesto was alarmed. His face was twisted in a grimace although he was not in pain. The grimace was for the pain he expected any moment.

"Tell me or I'll break your arm."

Ernesto looked into Sutton's eyes. He thought for a long moment and realized that Sutton was telling the truth. In another moment his arm would be broken and Sutton would ask once again where El Tigre lived.

Then, if he refused again, his other arm would be broken . . .

Not for a second did he consider calling for help. He knew instinctively that he would be dead long before any help could arrive. Sutton would kill him quickly and expediently and all the help in the world would help him not at all.

"He lives on La Calle de Barrios," Ernesto said in a very taut whisper. "It is a mile, perhaps two miles from the town. It is to the east."

"How do I get there?"

Ernesto told him. He made his directions as detailed and explicit as possible because he knew that Sutton would kill him if his directions were inadequate. He hoped that Sutton would remember the directions and arrive at the house of El Tigre.

After that he did not care what happened. The fool Sutton

would probably be shot dead for his troubles but this was no concern of Ernesto's. The sole concern of Ernesto was Ernesto, and for this reason he spoke clearly but quickly and gave flawless directions.

When he had finished Sutton released him. Sutton stood up and looked down at Ernesto, who remained on the bench and rubbed his arm where Sutton had been holding it. The arm did not hurt at all but Ernesto rubbed it anyway.

"You better be right," Sutton said.

Ernesto said nothing.

"If you're lying I'll come back and kill you with my bare hands."

"I know," Ernesto said.

Item one—find El Tigre.

That item had been taken care of. He knew where El Tigre was, knew so well from Ernesto's instruction that he could have drawn a map of the route. It wouldn't have been difficult—all he would have to do was close his eyes and copy the map that was etched across his brain. It would remain like that until he arrived at the house and it required no conscious memory work to hold it in place.

So much for item one.

Item two—get hold of something to kill the dirty bastard with.

Like what?

He had his hands, of course, and it would be a pleasure to use his hands to murder El Tigre, to catch a throat between two hands and to twist and squeeze until a life had been extinguished. Or to chop with the flat of his hand, or to dig his bunched fingers into the solar plexus and grope for the heart.

A pleasure.

Also a luxury that he could not afford. Because he only had one shot at El Tigre, just one chance which, if passed up, would result in his own death. His death was unimportant, but it would also bring about the failure of his mission. And his mission was important, very important.

So his hands would not be the weapon. The same line of thought ruled out a knife or a club. It was too risky and would force him to work too close to the man.

Therefore: Item two—get a gun.

He couldn't buy one because he had no money.

He couldn't borrow one because he didn't know anyone who owned one. He couldn't lift one from a shop because the shops were closed for the night.

He had to take one away from somebody who had one.

Therefore: Item two—grab somebody's gun.

From the park he headed east in the general direction of El Tigre's home. Specifically, the route he chose led him through the region that the native Mexicans referred to as Boy's Town. It was the few square blocks of cribs, one-room shack after one-room shack after one-room shack, block after block of them with the monotony of it spoiled by an occasional gin mill. In front of each crib was an orange crate and on each orange crate a broken-down prostitute with makeup hiding the scars and wrinkles on her face and cheap perfume attempting to conceal the fact that she never bathed.

The women charged one dollar and they would do anything. The women were not old, not really, but years on their backs had taken their toll. Boy's Town was the end of the line.

He did not want a woman or a drink. He did not want any of the delights available in Boy's Town, but he chose the area because he knew that the police patrolled it constantly. He wanted to encounter a policeman.

The police carry guns.

And Sutton was looking for a gun.

Therefore: Item two—take a gun away from a Mex cop.

CHAPTER 12

When he passed the shack the woman smiled at him, grabbed at his arm. When he turned and looked at her she saw that he was not looking for a woman, that even if he was he was the sort of man who could look at her in such a way and also want her, then she did not want his business. He was a man with death in his eyes, death or something worse than death, and she knew that if he made love to her he would give her a beating that would outweigh the dollar or two he would pay her. She was in no mood to be beaten and she let go of his arm quickly and, when he had passed, crossed herself. She did not understand why she crossed herself—she was not a religious woman, not especially, and now that he had passed she had nothing to fear. But she could not help feeling that she had looked upon the countenance of the Devil.

As for Sutton, he forgot her the moment she let go of his arm.

Item two—take a gun away from a Mex cop.

He kept on walking, knowing that the area was loaded with police and that he would run into one sooner or later. They were always around when you didn't want them, he thought, and never around when you did. For the first time in his life Sutton wanted a cop and he couldn't find one.

When he passed the saloon called La Buena Suerte and

rounded the corner he found a cop. He was so intent upon finding a cop that he identified the one he found just as a cop, and it
was several seconds before he realized that he knew the man. His
name was Ramon Calientes and Sutton knew him.

Ramon Calientes saw Sutton, recognized him and smiled.
He walked over with the friendly greeting of a friendly cop for
a friendly vagrant. The two were, in a sense, old friends. Once or
twice Ramon Calientes had bought a round or two of drinks;
twice or three times Calientes had taken Sutton to a comfortable
cell when Sutton was without a place to sleep and it was raining.

Ramon Calientes was not a young man. He had been a sergeant in the Mexican army for many years, and while the Mexican
army had little to do for the most part a man could still serve as
a sergeant for only so many years. When he was old there was no
room for him, and the Mexican army had a different system of
pensions than the army north of the border. Army men due to be
put to pasture were made policemen. The salaries were small but
the bribes were good enough to support a man and his family, a
faithful servant like Ramon Calientes who harmed no one and
who had worked diligently at a useless post in a useless army.

"My friend," Ramon Calientes, who spoke flawless English,
said. "You are sober. What is the matter?"

Sutton grinned mechanically. The light, he thought, was too
bright on the corner. That particular spot would not do. He
glanced around and saw the alleyway at the side of the Buena
Suerte. It was dark, quiet. No one ever walked through it because the drainage was bad and in the rainy season it was usually
swampy. In the dry season it was pitted with deep ruts and there
were easier footpaths available.

"Walk with me," Sutton said. "I have something to discuss with you."

He took the policeman's arm and led him to the alleyway. Ramon Calientes could not imagine what Sutton wished to discuss with him but he did not question his friend, the poor Americano who drank all the time. Ramon Calientes was a good man, a peaceful man, an infinitely patient man. He let himself be led into the alleyway.

"What is it, my friend?"

Five words. Simple words, soft words.

They were the last words Ramon Calientes ever spoke.

Sutton's fist caught him in the chest directly over the heart. The old man clutched himself and doubled over. Then Sutton chopped him with the flat of his hand on the side of the neck and the policeman fell to the ground. He did not moan, did not make a sound. Only the gentle sound of a body falling to the earth was heard and it was noticed by no one.

Sutton bent over, examined the man. Ramon Calientes was unconscious. Sutton found the pistol in its holster and unclasped the holster. He took the pistol and looked at it, smelled it, handled it. God knew how long it had been since the policeman had fired it if indeed he had ever fired it at all. Sutton broke open the gun, counted the six bullets, closed the gun and hefted it in his hand. Then he knelt again at the policeman's side.

Ramon Calientes had never harmed anyone. Now he was unconscious, harmless. Sutton could step over his body and leave to murder El Tigre and Calientes could do nothing to stop him. Afterward Calientes might catch him if he was not caught by others, but afterward was unimportant.

But, Sutton thought, there was no telling how long the old man would remain unconscious. There was no telling how long it would be before Sutton had his chance to kill El Tigre. There was the possibility, a dim possibility but an undeniable one, that Ramon Calientes might endanger the completion of Sutton's mission.

That could not be chanced.

Accordingly Sutton rolled Calientes over onto his back. He looked at him for just a second, took note of the even breathing and the relaxation of the tired old face in sleep.

Then, holding the pistol by the barrel, he raised the gun and brought it down so that the butt of it struck the policeman's head at the bridge of the nose. The first tap was gentle and was done more to enable Sutton to get the range than anything else.

The second blow cracked the skull of Ramon Calientes, caved in the skull and drove a piece of the frontal bone into the policeman's brain. He died instantly.

Sutton stood up. He was not even breathing hard and he was somewhat surprised. He bent down again to wipe off the butt of the gun on the policeman's uniform and realized that he had just killed a man, a man whom he had known personally, a man who had been his friend. He had never borne any ill will toward Ramon Calientes, never disliked him in the least. The cop was as good a friend as Sutton had in the world.

And Sutton had killed him.

He stood up again, slipped the gun into his pants pocket and left the alley. No one passed him, no one knew of the killing and no one suspected anything. Ramon Calientes might be covered with Sutton's fingerprints but that was not very important. It would take a long time before Sutton was ever caught by the fingerprints. By that time he would either succeed or fail and capture would be quite irrelevant.

A man was dead and he had killed him. He thought about that as he left Boy's Town and started toward Calle de Barrios. The map of the route to El Tigre's house was still etched upon his brain and he followed the route without looking at street signs, without counting the blocks and without thinking where he was going. It was as though his feet were following a path they had known for years, as though he was walking in his old neighborhood in the town where he had been born and as though he could walk forever without getting lost and without losing his trail.

Ramon Calientes was dead.

Sutton had killed him.

He did not regret it. He had liked Calientes when the man was alive and respected his memory now that he was dead, but the power to regret an action was no longer a part of his make-up. The death of Calientes was a part of an overall plan of operations. Whether it was a necessary step or not did not matter. It was a step that might turn out to be necessary and that was enough.

Calientes died because he had to die. Calientes died because El Tigre had to die. Sutton did not regret the fact or rejoice in it. He merely accepted it.

Item one, he thought. Find El Tigre.

And he knew where El Tigre was.

Item two—get a gun.

The pistol was in his pocket.

There was only one item left.

CHAPTER 13

On the road in front of the house of El Tigre there was a clump of brush hiding a ditch. In the ditch Sutton was crouching, his body tense, his nerves on edge. He had arrived. He was in front of El Tigre's home and the man he had to murder was only yards away.

He had come a long way. From a compartment at the sex show to the house of El Tigre, from the oblivion of alcohol to the keen excitement of vengeance. A corpse lay heavily on the path he had walked, the corpse of a man who had been his friend.

The corpse was forgotten.

The problem, now, seemed to be a simple one. All he had to do was enter the house, find El Tigre and blow his brains out with a bullet from the gun in his pocket. But Sutton saw that it was not as simple as it seemed. For one thing, a guard blocked the approach to the house.

The guard was standing relatively still a few steps from the front door. He wore no uniform and carried no visible weapon but he was as obvious a guard as the Grenadiers at Buckingham Palace. Sutton knew that it was the man's job to make sure that people like Sutton did not get inside of the house.

Therefore the guard was an obstacle.

The obstacle could, of course, be circled, Sutton could sneak around the guard and try to gain access to the house by route of a rear entrance. Instinct warned him against such a move and when he thought about it for a minute he ruled it out. If there was a back door—and a man who lived El Tigre's life would most certainly want more than one escape route—if there was such a door, it was undoubtedly guarded as well as the front door. More important, there was quite possibly some sort of alarm device that would reveal the presence of an intruder in the yard.

Sutton could see the route he could take very well now. The sun was coming up and the sky was bright. But he couldn't be sure that he could get around the house without tripping over a hidden wire. And that could be fatal.

No, he would have to get by the guard. He was no more than twenty or thirty yards from the man and he looked him over very carefully, noticed the way the man stood very still and did not even look around from side to side. Perhaps Sutton could sneak up on him. The guard looked tired, worn out, exhausted.

Perhaps . . .

Slowly, cautiously, Sutton crawled to the left side of the ditch. He raised his head again and studied the guard, who had not moved while Sutton was crawling to his left. Very carefully Sutton climbed out of the ditch and approached the guard from the back. The noises of early morning covered his footsteps—motor cars rumbled in the distance and birds sang in trees.

Sutton kept moving.

Miguel Mosca was twenty-three years old. He was a small young man with wiry muscles and a deep nut-brown complexion. His eyes were a brown that was almost black and his eyebrows were thick and bushy.

He would have been very surprised to know that a man was approaching him from the rear.

At the moment he was not thinking of men who approached people from the rear. His thoughts had nothing to do with the rather boring job of guarding El Tigre. On the contrary, his thoughts were a good deal more pleasant.

He was thinking of a girl.

Very few young ladies in towns like Nueva Laredo are at all respectable. The economic pursuits of the town make it such a place that young ladies are generally prostitutes. If a girl is poorly shaped or ugly to look upon she may become a waitress or a barmaid or a clerk, but such girls are the exception.

The girl of whom Miguel Mosca was thinking was very beautiful and was not a prostitute, which made her a definite exception. She had, in fact, been a virgin at the time Miguel married her almost a year ago, a fact which made quite an impression on Miguel who had not believed that there was a single virgin over the age of thirteen in the entire town of Nueva Laredo.

Now she was no longer a virgin. Now she was Miguel's wife and the mother of a son with the appetite of his father. Now she was at home waiting for her husband and he was tallying the minutes until he could be with her in their bed and take her into his arms and make love to her.

Soon, he thought, they would be able to leave Nueva Laredo. His job was perfectly respectable and highly profitable but he did not want to work for a man like El Tigre any longer. It was true that all he did was stand guard, but Miguel was a highly moral young man and the thought of guarding a bad one like El Tigre was at times a disturbing thought. It was in one sense a job like any other; in another sense, and Miguel's eyes, it was a distasteful job.

But soon there would be enough money in the small basket which Rosa Mosca kept under the bed, enough so that he and Rosa and Juan might leave Nueva Laredo and move to Monterrey. In Monterrey Juan could go to school and Miguel could get a job in the big factory. It was true that he would earn less money at first but it would be a pleasure to trade Nueva Laredo for Monterrey.

Miguel Mosca thought about it, about living in Monterrey with his wife and his son. He thought perhaps too much about it, thought too diligently about the pleasures he and Rosa and Juan would have.

If he had kept his mind on the job at hand he might have heard Sutton at the start. If he had been concentrating on guarding the house instead of planning his future he would have paid attention to the twig that he heard snap. As it was he did nothing. He did not even turn his head, but waited motionless in his tracks while his mind planned the future,

He only half-heard the whirr of the pistol as it descended, butt forward. And even then he was too involved in his own thoughts to react at all before the butt of the pistol had caved in the back of his skull.

The fact that the door was locked made no difference at all. There was a pane of glass in the door and once he had broken the glass it was a simple matter to reach through, turn the lock and open the door. No one seemed to hear the breaking of the glass. There was an old trick of holding a piece of cloth up to the window and then smashing it with a brick; Sutton compromised by ripping the shirt from Miguel's back and holding it against the window, then smashing the glass with his pistol butt. It worked neatly enough.

He was inside now and the hard part seemed to be over. Now it was time to get it over, to find the bastard and put a bullet in him. He didn't know which room in the huge house might be the one in which El Tigre lay sleeping—for that matter he couldn't be sure that the bastard was home. But, just as he sensed that the man was home, he also sensed that his bedroom was on the first floor. And by a quick process of elimination he decided on a door. He walked to it, stood in front of it. The stage was set. All he had to do was throw open the door and begin shooting.

He drew the gun and held it tight in his hand. The second finger curled around the trigger, the palm was moist with sweat where it came into contact with the gun butt. He looked for several long seconds at the weapon and then reached for the door knob.

His hand froze in mid-air when he heard someone moving on the second floor.

She was afraid.

She didn't know why. But suddenly she woke up, her face taut with fear and her hands trembling. El Tigre had left her and she was alone, and all of this was very frightening to her. She had a terrible premonition of danger, danger not to herself but to her man, and she wanted to be with him.

Now she was out of bed, her blonde hair hanging loose and untidy, her body warm from the bed. She slipped a robe on and opened the door of her room, then took a hesitant step into the hallway.

It was crazy. He would be mad at her, and beat her for interrupting his sleep over nothing,

But still . . .

She walked slowly to the head of the stairs. Her heart was pounding and her hands were trembling worse than ever but she didn't know what to do about it. He would be angry, terribly angry. He undoubtedly had a woman with him and if she came in at the wrong moment there would be hell to pay. At the very least she would get a terrible beating. More probably he would kill her, and if she knew him he would not kill her quickly and cleanly. Death would come slowly, horribly, and the thought made her tremble more and caused her heart to pound still harder.

It was ridiculous, she decided. Ridiculous to risk even a beating for nothing. She stood at the head of the stairs and listened very carefully but could hear nothing, no movement, no breathing.

Go to sleep, she told herself. And, obediently, she went back to the bedroom and closed her door. The tension flooded out of her the moment her head hit the pillow and she slept like a log.

He couldn't wait any longer. The footsteps upstairs had receded and a door had been closed. He was as safe as he would ever be and he had to act fast.

He took the door knob in his hand, twisted it and shoved the door open. Sunlight flooded the room through the open window and he could see very clearly the two bodies in the round bed. There was a man and a woman and they were lying quite nude in each other's arms.

Sutton closed the door. Then he turned around again and raised the pistol.

He took several steps closer to the bed. He had not fired a gun in a long while and, while he was very confident of himself just then, he wanted to make sure that he did not miss. He might not get many chances. The gun might misfire. There were too many things that could go wrong and he wanted to minimize their importance.

When he took the third step the man woke up.

El Tigre moved like a tiger, like a cobra, like greased lightning. He reacted instinctively, sensing only that there was an extra presence in the room and that this foreign presence represented a danger.

He did not sit up. Instead he uncoiled. He had been lying face down with his head pressed to the girl's breast but when he moved he turned and spun to his feet in one smooth and rhythmic motion.

He was on his feet, crouching, facing Sutton. Then Sutton's finger tightened on the trigger and the gun went off. The bullet caught El Tigre in the center of his face a quarter-inch below the nose. The bullet was a .45 caliber slug with a soft nose and it had a mushroom effect. It made a large hole on the way in and a larger one on the way out. It carried half of El Tigre's head across the room and sprayed the bed with blood and flesh and shreds of bone.

In the little room it sounded like a cannon.

Chapter 14

A body fell to the floor. It seemed to fall in slow motion and Sutton thought that hours passed before the corpse was lying in a human puddle on the floor at the side of the bed. He stood in his tracks with the smoking gun clenched tight in his hand and his eyes focused on the body at his feet.

Then he noticed the girl.

She was awake now.

She had seen him. She knew that he had killed, that El Tigre was dead and that Sutton had fired the shot that killed him. She could call for help or inform the police, and it was obviously essential to kill her too. He raised the gun again and pointed it at her and her eyes flickered from his face to the gun and back to his face again. She seemed totally unexcited about the gun that was aimed at the tip of her nose.

The policeman.

The guard.

Those deaths had been necessary. Those deaths were part of the plan, the mission, but now the plan had been finished and the mission was over with.

He could not kill the girl.

Slowly he lowered the gun, put it back in his pocket. His body went limp then but somehow he remained on his feet. Already his eyes were beginning to cloud over.

"Go ahead," he told the girl. "Call for help. Yell for the police. Go ahead, I won't hurt you, yell for help because I killed him. Go ahead."

The girl did not understand a word of English. If she had it would have made no difference. She still would have done just what she did now.

She smiled, a soft and lazy smile.

She rolled over on her belly and buried her face in a pillow.

And Conchita Perez went back to sleep.

He did not know, of course, that Conchita Perez could not be more grateful to him for killing the man she hated. He could not know this any more than he could know that this particular room was thoroughly soundproofed and that no one had been able to hear the shot. These were things which he could not and did not know, and all he did know was that somehow he managed to leave the room and the house undetected. Shortly afterward the day guard arrived to find the dead and shirtless body of Miguel Mosca, but by that time Sutton was already back in town.

He went directly to his room. The room was the same filthy hovel as it had been when he had left it some seventeen or eighteen hours ago. Filthy clothing covered the floor and paint was missing from the walls. But the room, he knew, was his home.

He was comfortable in it.

Mechanically he undressed and stretched out on the mattress. Then and only then did he fully realize that it was over, that he had done it, that he had managed to kill El Tigre. For a period of several hours he had been a man possessed, possessed by God or the Devil and he was not sure which.

It was over.

The full impact of it hit him in the head and he was suddenly too exhausted to move. Total physical exhaustion washed over him in a flood and every muscle went limp, every nerve stopped sensing, every coil of his brain ceased the strange physical process of thought. His eyes were closed, his brain was numb, his body was incapable of any activity whatsoever.

He slept.

He did not dream.

When he awoke he needed a drink so desperately that he could barely walk to the nearest bar . . .

Go to Nueva Laredo. You'll like it there—it's a paradise for the modern American.

By all means go there. El Tigre is dead, of course, but his death didn't alter the basic make-up of the thriving metropolis across the Rio Grande. You, as a tourist, will be a part of their basic industry. You, as a tourist, will enjoy yourself.

You may take drugs there, if you so desire. You may drink rum or tequila at very low prices. You may have any form of active or passive sexual activity that your stomach and wallet will permit.

It's an even money that your Diners' Club card will be good at the decent cathouses.

Don't miss Nueva Laredo. You'll love every minute of it, and you may meet some very interesting people. There are, of course, some that you won't meet. El Tigre is dead, as are Ramon Calientes and Miguel Mosca. But you would probably never have met El Tigre anyway, and you'd have found the policeman and the guard rather dull company.

You may run across Ernesto—he still works the park and produces a license which certifies that he is empowered to guide you to any form of aberration that suits your personal psyche. He and Conchita Perez are the only two persons in the world who know that Sutton killed El Tigre and they aren't telling.

You might meet Conchita, for that matter. You might take her to bed.

Or, if you're looking for someone to take to bed, there's always Mona Sutton. Although she's an American it will be hard for you to recognize her, for the sun has browned her face and body and the life she leads has turned her skin to leather. But if you walk among the cribs of Boy's Town long enough you'll probably run into her.

She's insane, of course. She no longer speaks English and what Spanish she jabbers in is incoherent and meaningless. But she will do anything in the world for a dollar.

Anything.

And if what you have in mind is something that will cause her pain, she will not mind. She even welcomes the pain. If you are looking for a woman to beat she is the obvious choice. The beatings remind her of a time that seems much longer ago than it was, a time when she was beaten and humiliated regularly by the only man she ever loved.

•   •   •

And, if you're very lucky, you may meet George Sutton.

Sutton is dying. He drinks every day, drinks more and more bad wine every day, and in time the wine will kill him. He knows this and he does not care.

Sutton is a man who literally got away with murder.

He is a man who, for a period of five or six hours, became a great man. For that length of time he was strong and brave and utterly fearless. For that length of time nothing in the world could stand in his way.

He killed three people, a policeman and a guard and a bad man. He killed them and he escaped—the crimes are listed officially as unsolved, and the Mexican police have never been famous for solving crimes unless the criminal is caught on the spot. They are mostly old men, faithful old soldiers like the late Ramon Calientes. In Nueva Laredo the long arm of the law has its hand outstretched palm upward. These men take bribes well, but they have not caught Sutton and never will.

And so Sutton lives on, sleeping in the same room, wearing the same rags, drinking bad wine bought with nickels and dimes and quarters which he receives from the tourists. There have been no Princeton men to treat him to good Scotch and good sex but Sutton does not mind. Wine is good enough for him and it will do for him until it kills him.

If you see him, buy him a drink. He deserves it. He is a bum now but for five or six hours he was a great man, and that's five or six hours more than most of us have.

And even if you don't meet Sutton, even if you never meet any of these people, your time will be well spent in the bustling little beehive that goes by the name of Nueva Laredo. You'll have fun there. Hell, everybody has fun there. You can't miss.

It's just the greatest place going.

My Newsletter: I get out an email newsletter at unpredictable intervals, but rarely more often than every other week. I'll be happy to add you to the distribution list. A blank email to lawbloc@gmail.com with "newsletter" in the subject line will get you on the list, and a click of the "Unsubscribe" link will get you off it, should you ultimately decide you're happier without it.

Lawrence Block has been writing award-winning mystery and suspense fiction for half a century. You can read his thoughts about crime fiction and crime writers in *The Crime of Our Lives*, where this MWA Grand Master tells it straight. His most recent novels are *The Girl With the Deep Blue Eyes*; *The Burglar Who Counted the Spoons*, featuring Bernie Rhodenbarr; *Hit Me,* featuring Keller; and *A Drop of the Hard Stuff,* featuring Matthew Scudder, played by Liam Neeson in the film *A Walk Among the Tombstones.* Several of his other books have been filmed, although not terribly well. He's well known for his books for writers, including the classic *Telling Lies for Fun &f Profit,* and *The Liar's Bible.* In addition to prose works, he has written episodic television (*Tilt!*) and the Wong Kar-wai film, *My Blueberry Nights.* He is a modest and humble fellow, although you would never guess as much from this biographical note.

Email: lawbloc@gmail.com
Twitter: @LawrenceBlock
Facebook: lawrence.block
Website: lawrenceblock.com

www.ingramcontent.com/pod-product-compliance
Lightning Source LLC
Chambersburg PA
CBHW060944180626
46817CB00004B/1699

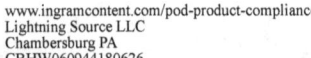